Lucian

McCray Bruin Book 1

KATHI S. BARTON

World Castle Publishing, LLC
Pensacola, Florida
Copyright © Kathi S. Barton 2018
Paperback ISBN: 9781949812527
eBook ISBN: 9781949812534
First Edition World Castle Publishing, LLC, December 24, 2018
http://www.worldcastlepublishing.com

Licensing Notes
Cover: Karen Fuller
Editor: Maxine Bringenberg

Chapter 1

Demi didn't care for the job she was doing. Not that she hated it, but she didn't like having to sneak in to keep an eye on her employees. They were an all right bunch, she supposed — for the most part anyway. But the shrink rate here was really high, and that meant someone was walking out the door with a great deal of food nightly. She was going to catch them, fire whoever it was, and have them arrested.

She heard the phone ringing in the distance and ignored it. No one knew who she was, neither here nor where she lived. They thought her name was Cassie Jones — best she could come up with — when she was really Demetrius Morgan. No one here called her Demi, however, which she'd gone by for nearly twelve years now.

Spraying off the dishes that had come back from the dining room, she noticed that the people seemed to be eating all their food. What was left over wasn't enough to make a twenty-seven percent shrink rate. Someone whistling had her turning toward the doorway to where she was working.

"Your name Demetrius Morgan?" Before she could think to say no, he nodded when she told him it was. "Okay, didn't know that, but you have a phone call. Said it's important."

Going to the very public phone, she tried to think who might have been calling her. No one. No one other than a couple of people knew her real name and knew where she was, and no one had called her by her first name since she'd left home.

"Who the fuck is this?" She kept her voice down but let the fury that she had right now show though. The voice on the other end sputtered and stammered. "Who the fuck is calling me here and knows anything about me?"

"Ms. Morgan? I'm so sorry to have bothered you there, but you're very difficult to find. My name is Daxton Peyton." She asked him what reason he could have for trying to find her. "Your mother, miss. She's passed away."

"And? You want me to do a jig? I will if necessary. But right now, I want answers. Why are you contacting me?" He repeated that her mother had passed away, three months ago as a matter of fact. "Again, that gave you no right to contact me. It's not like we were even on the worst of terms. I hated her as much as she did me. And the same for my sister and brother. Why are you looking for me anyway? I'm sure that she had no more use for me than I did her."

"She was buried three months ago, and I've been trying to locate you since. As I said, you've proven to be very difficult to find. There is a will. You're named in it, as are your sister, Ms. Astrid Morgan Chase, and your brother, Mr. Nathan—"

"I fucking know who they are. What did you hope to gain by contacting me? And if you tell me again how hard it was to find me, then think on that for a moment. Perhaps that was because I had no desire to be found, you moron." She looked around the kitchen and realized that they'd stopped working to stare at her. She decided it was time to come clean on a few things. "Look, I'll contact you in a couple of days, no sooner. If you pester me, I'll simply get lost again. Just give me your contact information and I'll call you when I have a few minutes."

"All right. But your family is getting upset that you can't be found so the will can be read." Rolling her eyes, she thought of all the things she could tell this man, but only asked again for his phone number. "Thank you."

"I don't want your thanks, Mr. Peyton, I want you to leave me the fuck alone." He said again that he was sorry, but that this was important. "Not as important as my privacy. Goodbye."

She hung up the phone and stood there, leaning her head against the wall the phone was on. Demi wanted to go home, call this man, and give him a piece of her mind. Or sue him. She didn't know what for, but she wanted him to pay for making her name a public format.

Before she could say anything to those around her, she was touched on the arm and then dragged into the offices. The chef, Daniel Westbrook, told her to sit down. She did. Demi was much too exhausted right now to think that she was his boss.

"Demetrius Morgan. That's you." She said it was. "You sign our checks. I'm assuming that you have a good reason for doing a shit job when you own this place. Probably more than this place."

"I do. On both points. The restaurant is losing money. I think that someone is stealing food. I was seeing if I could find

7

out who was doing it before the police were brought in." He nodded and asked if she had ruled him out. "I've not ruled anyone out just yet. I think that someone in your kitchen and a waitstaff person is doing it. But I can't tell how."

"I guess I'll have to take that as a good sign. But they're not taking shit while I'm here. And I have noticed someone going out of here with a bag full of stuff. I'm assuming that you've not checked your email in a couple of days." She said she'd been busy. "I bet you have. I was letting you know that a big portion of the meat we had delivered is missing. Steaks, roasts. A lot of meat, and some vegetables."

"Seven hundred pounds of beef, two hundred of pork, and a few hundred chickens. If vegetables are missing, I haven't found that yet." He pulled out the inventory that she'd gotten three days ago. "I have this."

"Yes, but I'm been keeping a daily tab on things. Also, I've been taking pictures of the locker room when I leave at night and when I come in. I asked you, in the email, if I could install a camera." She flushed and said she was sorry. There was really no need for the camera, she thought. Demi sort of had an idea who was doing it. "No need to be. You had no way of knowing who you could trust, and I'm glad that you didn't come in here and start accusing anyone. Or making me responsible for what's going on."

"I'm not like that." He handed her the second sheet. This one had daily columns with a total each day. Then he told her the highlighted areas were trucks coming in. "So, whoever they are, they're hitting us right after the truck comes in."

"Pretty much. And since I have to be here for the truck, the things coming out of it are dead on. Nothing shady with them." She grinned at him. "Something else I should know?"

"I own them too—at least the shipping company. I had a shake down a few months ago with them about missing inventory. They're very good now with making sure customers get what they should have." He laughed. "I might have to go out of town for a few days. I have personal business that I have to deal with."

"I heard. No one else would have—I kept them away. But I'm not human, as I'm sure you know." She nodded, still going over the inventory. "Ms. Morgan, I'm sorry about your loss."

"Don't be. We were never close. And since she passed away, I have to be there now." She looked up at him. "I'm extremely private, Daniel. Any of this gets circulated around, and I will make your life not worth living. I can promise you that."

"I believe you." She handed him the paperwork and asked him if he'd keep an eye on things until she returned. She told him that she'd call him in a couple of days with a burner phone. "All right. Is there anything I can do in the meantime?"

"Stay out of it. You're not to engage, even if you find out. And I'll have cameras installed at the back door and the locker room. If something happens that I can catch, you'll never know—not until a few employees stop showing up." He asked her why she thought it was more than one person. "It would take a lot of muscle to carry out that much meat. One of the female employees could probably do it, but none of them drive a car big enough to carry it away. There are four trucks on the lot, yours and mine not included. One of your chop help might be doing it, but he's too frail to have me believe that he's doing this alone. At this point, I'm not ruling

9

anyone out but you."

Demi went to her home and packed some things that she might need for the next week. She wasn't naïve enough to think that this would only take a day or two. Her family never did anything quickly, nor like she wanted them to. She made arrangements to fly out in the morning and called the man who was going to replace her in the restaurant to let him know he needed to show up.

"I was going to ask you. I liked being at home all the time at first, but now I'm bored." Demi told him that she'd gotten the other job, the ploy that she'd used to get him to take a few days off. "Thanks so much for this. My wife sure did enjoy having me home a bit more. But she, too, is ready for me to go back."

After squaring away the rest of the house, she went to her office. Demi pulled up her mother's name to see if she really was dead. The headline said all she needed to know — Abrielle Morgan had passed away after a bout with the flu. It went on to mention that she had two daughters and one son. No names were mentioned, not even her beloved Astrid and Nathan's, but she had been buried next to Demi's father a few days after she'd passed away.

Demi tried very hard not to think about her family. They hadn't ever thought of her, she was sure. When she'd left home, she'd been just shy of her seventeenth birthday — seven days after graduating at the top of her class in high school, and only mere hours away from graduating at the top of her class in college.

Not only did she speak several languages, but she also had a degree in business management and a minor in accounting. When she had left home, Demi had set herself up in a house with the money she'd horded, as well as finished her education to become the best that she could be. Now years later she had a doctorate in business management, and also one in history. Education had always been a priority for her—never to her family. Demi remembered well the argument that she'd had and the physical fight that ensued the day she'd left.

"You're not going." Her mother didn't answer her. Her graduation from college, much more important than high school, was coming up and her mother was still in her pajama's. Abrielle, as she'd been told to call her mother, had only told her that she didn't feel inclined to go to anything she was doing. "I see. So, if this had been Nate or Astrid, you'd be right there with them."

"Of course. You were never any kind of favorite of mine, and I can't believe that since you've managed to fuck your way to a diploma, you'd think things would change for you. I want you out of this house as soon as I can manage it. You're what, four years from turning eighteen? I'll have you out the door so fast when you turn that magic number that you'll not even touch the grass that is *my* front yard."

"I'm seventeen now. I'll be eighteen in two months." Her mother said that was wonderful news. "You've never cared for me, have you, Abrielle? Not one bit."

"Never. Had I found out that I was carrying you sooner, you wouldn't be anything but a drop in some quack's bucket. As it was, I couldn't very well send you to some ass hold that would buy you from me either, since that old bat knew you were around." Her grandmother; her father's mother, Milly Morgan. "She's the only reason that I've not had you killed off."

Grandma Morgan had been the one to tell her to leave the

11

house. Demi had lived with her until she was fully recovered. The beating that she'd taken from first Nathan, then Astrid, had hospitalized her for several days, followed by bed rest for several weeks. No one had known she was there, and as far as she understood, they'd never asked about her either. It was just as well, Demi thought. It was the beginning of the end for her little family, and contact between them.

Grandma had died several weeks ago, and Demi had been the only family at the service. Grandma had given her so much over the years — money to help pay for college, money for a car when she needed one, and leaving her a house and her money when she passed away. Grandma Morgan had been the only one that had loved her, and now she too was gone.

Getting up the next morning, her head splitting from staying up too late. Demi boarded the plane and put her overnight in the overhead storage bin, taking her laptop to her seat with her. Settling in, Demi was happy that she'd purchased the seat next to her so that she could sit alone. People, she knew, would want to pass the time, and she had enough going on without making small talk with a stranger.

The plane took off on time, and she calculated how long it would take her to get to Ohio. She was going to stay in Grandma's house that she'd left her, and make sure that she had everything up to date in it. The house wasn't on the market yet — she wasn't even sure she wanted to sell it — but it would be nice when she decided what to do with it.

Renting a car at the airport, she drove to the house and parked in the massive garage. Grandma's staff had been informed that she was coming, so the house would be aired out and everything ready for her. The only staff that had stayed on after Grandma passed were her butler and cook. Demi figured that would be all she needed, since a cleaning crew came in once a week to do the dusting and such. Moses met her at the door with a list. After a tight hug, he told her what he'd done for her concerning her mother's funeral.

"I made arrangements with the attorney that contacted you. I'm so sorry, Demi. I had no idea it would take so long. I sent flowers to the funeral home, no name attached, and paid cash for it. I have also made sure that the bills were paid for the funeral. They had not been." Demi thanked Moses, an old sounding name for a man younger than her. "Additionally, there has been some talk about the children trying to sell off the family furniture. I think they were getting desperate for you to come home."

"Do you have any idea why I was named in the will?" Moses speculated that she was telling her off once and for all. "Could be. I don't think that she had a pot to piss in other than the insurance money that Dad left her, and the other two spent money like it was their job."

"The taxes haven't been paid on the estate or any of the credit cards that they managed to get. Which, by my estimation, is about five thousand dollars. Not much, but it is getting them hounded by the creditors. I have been able to purchase the controlling stock for you in the last few days of your grandmother's company, as you asked me to do. If you want to go over that, it's there on your desk." They were sitting at the kitchen table, a place where she and her grandma had eaten more than in the big dining room. "I've contacted your attorney, Mr. Shoe, and he is well aware that you're going to the reading of the will. He said that he'd be there with you. He believes that you'll need him."

13

"I guess I might." She ate some of the cupcakes that were on a tray before speaking again. "Now that Abrielle is gone, I might stick around here. Astrid and Nathan mean nothing to me, and even if they want something, I'm very good at telling people no. What do you think would happen should I move here?"

"I'd be happy, and I know that your grandma would as well. It's been too long since a Morgan has been living here." She nodded. "Demi, they're broke, and...and well, you're not. They're going to cause you some trouble wanting money from you."

"As I said, I'm really good at saying no. And I'm not that seventeen-year-old kid anymore. I've done a lot of growing up being on my own. Also, I've taken enough self-defense classes that I can hold my own now." He laughed and said that all she'd need to do was be able to walk fast. "I don't understand."

"They've gotten fat. I don't mean slightly overweight, but fat. I bet that Nathan weighs as much as four hundred pounds now. Not a good look on his short frame. And Astrid drinks too much and is as lazy as always. She more than likely weighs in at about three fifty." Demi laughed. "I saw them a few weeks ago, when they were here looking for you. Astrid still dresses like she's a teeny bopper, and Nathan wears stretchy shorts. Year round. He blames it on the stress of keeping the family together, but he hasn't done a day's work in all his life. Nor has Astrid for that matter."

They talked about this and that, mostly concerning the house, and once in a while they'd come back to her brother and sister. She hadn't known about them being heavy, but the rest she knew. Astrid had been married six times—divorced that many times too. She would marry up, as Grandma had called it, trying to find a man that would die soon and leave her everything. The only thing she'd been left was bills. No one would marry her without a prenup. That, Demi thought, had a great deal to do with her putting a little information on the table about her dear sister.

Nathan had been married twice, and both times the women had left him high and dry. He had a daughter that Demi made sure was safe from her father. Nathan also had more bills than his ass could cover. There were two houses that he was paying on, both left to his wives, as well as a car, credit cards, and a shit load of attorney fees for when he got himself into one kind of trouble after the other.

Her appointment had been moved from tomorrow, which she'd been planning on, to this evening. It was only one in the afternoon now, so she drove herself to the cemetery where Grandma was buried. Grandda was there too — his death had occurred before she was born.

Putting the flowers on their graves as she sat on the bench she'd had put in, she told them of her trip here. "I'm going to see them tonight. I'm not sure that I'm ready for that. I mean, I'm not stupid — I know that they're going to try and blame me for their lot in life — but I also know something that they don't. I have more money than they'll ever have." Demi told them both about her new business venture, as well as the problems she was having at the restaurant. Nothing she couldn't figure out, she assured them, but it was annoying. She told them too that her mother had passed away. But since they more than likely already knew that, she moved on. Demi looked out over the beautiful cemetery and wondered for a moment if she should visit her mother's grave. "I won't, just so you know. There was nothing between us in life, and there is less now that she's dead.

"I've been watching the stock market, as you taught me to do, Grandma. I have bought and sold more businesses than I think you and I did when you were around. I miss you, by the way. Bouncing ideas off of you while we talked was something that I looked forward to every time, and I miss that now." Kneeling down, she pulled a small weed out of the otherwise pristine flower garden that had been planted by her. "I have to see the attorney tonight. I'm not sure how he found me, but I intend to find out. I don't know what Abrielle wanted of me or why she would mention me in her will, but I'm guessing this is her way of letting Astrid and Nathan try and beat the crap out of me one more time."

It wouldn't work this time. Not only had she learned to defend herself, but she also had learned to carry and shoot a gun. There would be no more taking her to the floor and beating her to shit. No more stitches from them using their boots on her body. She was her own woman, and she would defend herself no matter what.

When it was time for her to leave, she kissed both headstones and told them she'd see them later. As she was leaving the cemetery, she wondered about the car parked just down from hers. But since no one had bothered her, she never paid it much mind.

Demi hated to be late and disliked it when other people were late too. She always made it so that she was early, so that she didn't have to worry about something befalling her to make her behind. And when she got to the offices of the attorney, she was told that Ms. Chase was running late and picking up Mr. Morgan. But Mr. Peyton popped his head out of an office and smiled at her.

"If you'd like to come on in, Demi, I'm sure you have questions." She nodded and stood up. "Your attorney called me today, just to make sure that you were represented should you need it. I assured him that you'd not need him this evening, as this was just a meeting, but that tomorrow he should be here."

"I want to know, first of all, how did you find me?" She was asked to have a seat. "Mr. Peyton, I don't want my name out there in the public. I'm sure that, if you've had any dealings with my family, you can understand why."

"I do. And they haven't any idea of anything about you other than that I found you. They've asked, I will admit to that, but I never told them anything. Not one thing." She nodded. "I put a search out to find you from some of my trusted friends in this business. It was difficult, I will say that for you. Even when I heard from Mr. Shoe, he wasn't easily willing to give me any contact information. He only gave me that number when the timing of the will was getting close."

"What does that mean?" He said that part would be explained tomorrow. "No, tonight, or I walk."

"I'd rather you didn't force my hand, Demi. And I know that I should ask to use such an informal name, but to think of you being associated with Astrid and Nathan makes my skin crawl." Mr. Peyton shivered. "How on earth are you from the same family? I shouldn't say that, but goodness, they are a pair, aren't they?"

"Yes, well, Abrielle wasn't any better."

The noise out in the hall made her aware that the pair in question had shown up, and with them all the noise, cursing, and even bodies being pounded against the walls. They walked in—waddled in was more like it—and she stood up. It was a defense thing—sitting down around these two would always get her hurt. But when Nathan smiled at her and Astrid sucked in her cheeks in an effort to make herself look thinner, she supposed, Demi knew that they had no idea who she was. Good, this might be more fun than she'd thought.

"Well, hello there, gorgeous. Had I known you were going to be here, I would have arrived on time." He winked at her as he turned to look at Peyton. "You didn't tell me that you hired someone to work for you, Dax. She sure is a looker."

"Sit down, you idiot. She's your sister. Demetrius arrived on time. Now we can get started. Your mother left each of you an envelope. You're not to open it until tomorrow when you come back here at one. She was very serious about this. If you bring the envelope back to me opened or tampered with, you forfeit some of the estate." He handed them all an envelope, and Demi put hers in her bag with all the other paperwork that she had to take care of in the morning. "All right. That's all for this evening. I will see you all tomorrow at one. Do not be late."

Mr. Peyton showed them out. Neither of her siblings spoke to her in the hall or the elevator ride down. It wasn't until they were in the lobby that Nathan drew back his fist and slammed her in the face. It had been too fast for her to do anything more than fall to the floor. That was the last thing she remembered except for the face of a man standing over her.

Chapter 2

Madden was going to stay with the woman until she was admitted. Her face was a mess, and she was going to need some surgery on her lip if she was ever going to be able to kiss again. Madden thought it would be a shame if she couldn't, since she was a pretty little thing. When the gun in her purse spilled out, he'd put it in his pocket so she'd not get herself into trouble. Had he been thinking, he might have used it on the man and the woman with him.

The man who had hit her had swung at him too, but since he wasn't a female and was faster on his feet, Madden had been able to knock the man out. The guy had ended up with a broken nose, four broken ribs, as well as a lip that was going to need a few stitches. Honestly, Madden wasn't sure why the man hadn't died of a massive heart attack before now. He was nothing but blubber.

"Madden, where are you, son?" He stood up and peeked around the curtain and waved at his dad. They'd been meeting for lunch, but when he'd gotten sidetracked with this, his dad had said he'd meet him here at the hospital. "Is she going to be all right?"

"The doctor said that she hit her head, and he wants to keep an eye on her. At least until she wakes up. Dad, that guy that hit her, he didn't say shit. Just swung around and hit her right on the mouth. Who does that?"

"A human. Your mom is coming in too. I told her that I had it, but she said that she wanted to make sure you weren't hurt. I don't know why she'd think that when you told her several times you were all right." Madden told him that she loved him. "I love you too, but I'm not going to go all mushy when you defend a damsel in dire need."

"It's distress, not dire need." The woman sat up, then laid back down. Her words were all mumbled because of her lip, but Madden understood her just fine. "Nathan never could go by me without slugging me. Where is he? Jail, I hope."

"Yes. I pressed charges for you—I hope you don't mind. But he hit me too. Jimmy, a local police officer, said that he's had trouble with him before. Is he your husband?" The woman told him that he was her brother. "Ah. And the woman with him, she's related to you as well. Sister?"

"Yes, unfortunately." Sitting up slowly, she accepted his help. "I need to get out of here before Astrid finds me. I'm in no position to deal with her antics today. Thank you for your help. I might not have survived this trip if not for you."

"It was my pleasure, miss." He waited for her to fill him in on her name, but she stood up and said nothing more. "My name is Madden McCray. This is my father, Alden. I'm sorry, but I didn't catch your name."

"That's because I didn't throw it at you. But I'm Demi Morgan. I'm here because Abrielle, my mother, passed away

20

some months ago." Madden looked at his father, then back at the girl. She must have felt some of their tension and turned to look at the two of them. "Something that I need to be aware of?"

"You're Milly Morgan's granddaughter." She smiled then, like she was lighting up the room when his dad asked about her grandma. "I knew her. Had I not been so worried about you, I might have recognized your face. You look just like her when she was just a young woman. My goodness. I'm sorry that she passed away. Not a greater person I knew as a young boy growing up."

"She was my savior and my world. And had it not been for her, I might not have survived my family when I lived here." Dad told her that he'd not realized she was related to Nathan and his sister. "Abrielle didn't like me. Actually, she loathed me. When I lived at home, I was either their punching bag or someone that would be thrown to the wolves when there was a problem. I spent more time in the hospital than I did in my bedroom. Which wasn't anything more than a space in the basement right next to the washer and dryer."

"I'm sorry, honey." She waved Dad off, telling him it was old news. But Madden could tell that it bothered Dad. Madden asked her what she was going to do now. "Yes, you'll need a ride someplace. I'm assuming that you're living at the homestead?"

"I am. I was thinking about opening the place up, maybe either living in it or selling it off. A great deal of my good memories come from that house." She signed herself out of the hospital and they made their way to Dad's car. It was a beater—all their cars were—but it ran well and had four doors. More than some had. "I'll need to go to the attorney,

21

Mr. Peyton's, office. I left my car there. And I need to find my gun."

"I have it. It's here." He handed it over to her and she put it in her purse after making sure that it was still loaded. Her weapon had probably cost more than he'd made all of last month. But Madden was glad that she had something to protect herself with. "You brought it with you to take care of yourself?"

"Yes, but it was already here at Grandma's house. I know how to use it, but I couldn't bring it on a plane." He nodded and watched her turn slowly in her seat. "I don't know if I can drive home now that I've been sitting up for a while. Perhaps you can just take me home, and I'll have Moses and his wife come back and get the car."

"I can drive you back. I don't have a car in town, so it won't be any trouble. And my dad can follow me over to pick me up." She looked at Dad and he nodded, saying it'd be no trouble at all. "That way, Mr. Moses won't have to come into town, and you'll still have your car."

"Thank you. I'm not used to having people helping me. I try very hard to do things on my own."

Madden could see that—she was very independent.

They swapped her out in her car and Madden had a few moments of worry. The car was brand new, and while it was a rental, as she told him, it was newer than anything he'd ever driven before. He should have thought this through, his mind told him, and when she asked him if he was all right, he turned to her.

"I'm not sure if you remember the McCrays, but we have been dirt poor and living on the edge of poverty since I was born. Before then I guess. This car.... Well, Ms. Morgan, it's well out of my realm of being able to replace it should I do something to it." She told him it was just a car. "To you, perhaps, but to me it's a luxury that I will never have. It even smells good."

"Thank you, Madden. I really appreciate you being honest with me. But as I said, it's just a car. One that I rented to get home. And there is insurance on it." She smiled at him. "I don't say this to many people, fewer than the fingers on one hand, but I trust you. Very much so. And while I believe you to be an excellent driver, the vehicle can be replaced."

They talked about her grandma on the way home. While Madden knew of her, he'd not been in the same social circles as the elderly woman. He didn't say that to Demi; he was positive that she'd rip him a new ass if he did. There was something about her, something that made him feel so protective of her, that he knew that she was different than any other woman he'd met.

"I don't want you to take this the wrong way, Madden, but I would like to hire you to keep me out of trouble. I make a great deal of it on my own, but I'm concerned that either one of my family might come after me again." She laughed a little. "Be my bodyguard for the next several days."

"I'd love to. But I have a job." She said that she understood. "You do know that I'm not human, right? I mean, I'm a shifter—bear, as a matter of fact."

"I do. My grandma, she knew of your family too. She didn't socialize much, not since I left home. She, too, was afraid of my family. And as frail and elderly as she was, they would have killed her had she been found alone." He said he was sorry. "Don't be. She did what she needed to do, went where she had to with Moses. He loved her as much as I did.

They were very good friends. And now he works for me. It was just a thought, anyway."

"My brother, Lucian, is out of work right now. The plant where he worked, the distribution center, it closed down when they opened up a new one a state over. It was hard on a lot of people. And had any of them had any kind of notice, I think it would have been easier to ease into another job. As it is now, there aren't any to be had around here." She asked him what Lucian had done there. "Shift manager. He was paid well, but the work is gone now. And because they didn't close up but moved, he's finding it hard to even get unemployment."

He could tell that she was hesitant. Demi didn't know Lucian, and she only trusted Madden through his saving her from being hurt too badly. While she thought about it, or whatever she might be doing, he reached out to his brother and asked him if he'd help out if she wanted.

Drive a new car to haul a woman around town? Sure. I'd be a fool to turn it down. But I'd like to meet her. If I have to spend any amount of time in a car with someone, I don't want her to be a bitch. Madden asked Lucian if he remembered Astrid. *Yes. Please tell me that it's not her. Nor is she related to her.*

Sister, believe it or not. But the thing is, she's absolutely nothing like her. Or nothing like Nathan. Untrusting, yes. She has that in spades. And with good reason. He told Lucian what had happened today. *I don't know what he might have done to her had I not been there, Lucian. He was out for blood. And someone as big as him, I'm surprised that he moved so quickly to hit her.*

Where can I meet her? Madden told his brother where they were headed. *All right. I'm not far from there. Let her know that I'm coming by if she's all right with that. And you hang around with me. That way I won't scare her. Sounds like she has had it bad*

24

if she's related to those two.

They pulled up in front of the house. It was beautifully maintained, and he was sure that it had been in her family for generations. Not like their home. It was a rental that they'd been living in since he'd been born. Madden had shared his room with two of his brothers, and it was tight. But now that he was out of the house, as were all of them, his living arrangements weren't that much better.

"I've contacted Lucian. He would like to meet you. And he said that if you trust him, he'll be glad to protect you." She nodded, staring out the window to the house. A man in a suit came out, but he didn't come to the car. "He's a good man, my brother. Just fallen on hard times."

"I'm sorry for that." She turned to him. "What is it you do, Madden? I mean, is it a good paying job? Do you like it? I would really like to know."

"I work at a factory that makes those plastic bowls and lids that are used in restaurants for take home stuff. Do I like it? No, I can honestly say that I don't care for it. But like it or not, I have to eat. And I send what I can to my parents." He looked in the rearview mirror and saw his brother in his truck rumbling up the drive behind their dad. "The pay sucks too. I mean, it's a living, but that's about all. I can live on it, but there isn't enough left over for an emergency."

He wondered why he was able to tell her this when he wasn't able to tell his parents the same thing. Not even his brothers knew just how he felt about his job. When she got out of the car, he did as well. Boy, to be able to ride around in something that wasn't as old as he was would be awesome. But he had a car, more than a lot of others in town had. And a roof over his head, food in his cabinets, as well as a coat when the weather turned cold.

When Lucian stopped to talk to their dad, he waited with Demi until they were finished. And when Dad and Lucian started toward them, Madden wanted to snatch up Demi and hide her away. He had no idea why he was so very protective of this stranger.

~*~

Lucian didn't want to frighten her. He'd had a long conversation with his buddy Jimmy and knew that this thing with her family had been going on since she'd been a tyke. It was terrible the way some people treated their family. His was the best there was, and he was glad every day that he had them.

When she paused at the car, he watched her while she watched him.

"I don't know you at all, do I?" He shook his head, not wanting to bring up that she'd been privileged and he'd not. "Don't do that. Don't judge me before you even know who or what I've been through. I can see it in your eyes, calculating how I have more than you do. Think of it this way, Mr. McCray—you have something that I've never had, and that money will never buy me. A family that cares for you and loves you no matter what."

"I'm sorry. I shouldn't have done that. You're right. I'm Lucian, not Mr. McCray please. You must be Demetrius Morgan. I know your brother, Nathan. If you don't mind me saying so, he's a piece of shit." She nodded and said she thought he was being generous with that. "Yes, well, my mom would box my ears if I said something bad about someone else's family."

"Yes, well, he is that and more. So is my sister. You know

26

her?" He said that he did but didn't have anything nice to say about her either. "It's doubtful that anyone would. I would like to hire you, Mr. McCray. I need someone to travel around with me to make sure that I'm— What's wrong with you?"

He didn't know what to do when her scent blew over him. He looked around, trying to figure out where to go to see if he was right. But her scent hit him right between the eyes like a ball would have. Moving a step forward, she took one back. His bear didn't like it any more than he did when Madden stepped closer to her.

"Madden, I can only ask you this once before I have to harm you. Please back away from Demetrius."

Madden got it. Not only did he move back, but he pulled Dad back from her as well. Demetrius moved forward and slapped him across the face. Lucian stood there, holding his hand over his injured cheek while he fought with his inner beast.

"What was that for?"

"You're scaring the fucking shit out of me, and I will not have you treating others like they should obey your every command. Now, whatever is going on, you can just deal with it. My sister is pulling up the driveway. If you can't conduct yourself like a grown man, then get in your car and get the hell out of here. I'll have enough to deal with without you acting like a moron."

He smiled. She sure was full of fire, and he loved it, even though she had given him a taste of it. Turning at the sound of the car stopping, he watched as the overweight woman struggled to get out of the car, a small, bright red compact. It was much too small for a woman her size and age. This was her sister? They couldn't have been more opposite, he

27

thought.

"Demi. So, you've stolen Grandma's house, have you? And even before the will is read. What a shame that you're not going to get to stay here for long. I'm claiming it for my own, just so you know. Then I'm going to fire those lazy fucks that are sucking up the air that I breathe." Dad moved up to stand next to him. Madden stood on the other side of Demi. "What the hell did you think you were doing, having some guy knock poor Nathan to the ground like he was nothing to you?"

"He is nothing to me. Neither are you, for that matter. What are you doing here?" Astrid looked him over. Lucian felt like meat on a hook and wanted to take a long hot shower. He wasn't even sure that would help his feelings of being dirty. "Keep away from these people, Astrid, or I swear to you, what happened to Nathan will be nothing compared to what I do to you."

"You're very brave for someone that has a fat lip and a black eye, sister dear. Have you opened your envelope? I have. She told me how I was her favorite, and that if I were to see you, I should treat you no differently than I did when we were children. That was fun times for us, wasn't it?"

Demi said nothing to her sister, and that, Lucian thought, was the best way to treat her. When she made a lunge-like threat to Demi she didn't even flinch, but it did make his family laugh. That made Lucian very proud to have her as his mate. He wasn't looking forward to telling Demi that, but he knew that she'd be safer now than she would have without any of his brothers.

Astrid laughed like she knew some big secret, but Demi wasn't having any of it—she just crossed her arms over her chest. Demi wasn't one to fuck with, and while Astrid's laughter made his bear roar at him to keep Demi safe, Astrid seemed to think it was a big joke and laughed again.

"I want you to get off my property." Astrid asked her how she thought it was hers. "Grandma left it to me and only me. If you think that it might have been part of Abrielle's estate, then you're in for a bigger disappointment than you might have imagined. This is mine."

"We'll see about that, won't we?" Astrid walked back to her car, nearly falling off the heels that should have been on someone much younger and lighter on her feet. When she paused and turned to look at her sister, Lucian tensed up, waiting for whatever Astrid said. "Tomorrow when we all meet again, you had better bring someone with you to pick up the pieces, Demi. You're going to be nothing but shit under my boot when I inherit it all and toss you to the dogs."

"Since you have nothing that I want, nor did your mother, then I have no idea why you think I'd care if you got it all. What I'd like to know is, why are you so sure that there is anything for you to get? I mean, last I heard, you were only a few cents from being tossed out on your collective asses anyway." The anger that spread over the distance between the sisters was palpable. Lucian watched, his bear ready to do whatever it took to keep her safe. "Go home, Astrid, while you still can. I don't want, nor do I need, anything that you think you might have."

Flipping Demi off, Astrid got into her car. Lucian knew that she was going to be stupid and try something else. So as soon as she revved up her engine, he stood in front of Demi so that she'd not be sprayed with the stones in the drive. The pelting at his back hurt, and he couldn't imagine what it would have done to Demi should she had been standing there.

"You can move now, she's gone." He just shook his head at Demi when she spoke softly. "Mr. McCray, I'm not in the mood to be bullied right now. And I'm barely hanging on. I'm an inch or so from falling flat on my ass, I'm so upset."

"I'll hold you." She nodded and turned. Lucian swept her up in his arms just as she started to fall. "I have you. Let's get you into the house and looked after. She will never bother you again."

Setting her on the couch, Lucian wasn't surprised that his brother and dad had come in with them. The butler — he said his name was Moses — handed him a full glass of an amber looking liquid that he put on the table beside Demi. Pushing her head between her knees, he was glad that she allowed him to do it.

Dad spoke quietly to Madden. He knew they were speculating on what was going on, and to be honest, so was Lucian. When Demi lifted her head up and looked at him, Lucian told her that she was his mate.

"Yes, I kind of figured that one out on my own when you got all macho out there. I don't need you as a mate, but I think I could get used to you hanging around." She put her fingers on her lip, and he sat up enough from his position on the floor to suckle the lower one into his mouth. He could taste the blood, and knew that she had to be in a great deal of pain. When he pulled back, the wound was healed and the swelling was going down too. "You fixed it. Thank you."

"You're welcome. And if you don't mind me saying so, you're taking this a good deal better than I thought you would." She asked him what good it would have done for her to be upset. "I don't know. None, I guess. We're mated and matched."

"Yes, well, I would like to think on that a bit. I'm not one to move forward quickly on anything. It's not my style." He asked her what her style was. "I think on things, move around my thoughts, and try and figure out what is the best course of action to take before I lose my ass. I never take chances with my heart or my money."

"I'm about as broke as a man can be right now." She shook her head and leaned back on the couch. He had no idea how she knew that Moses had returned, but she asked him to please call Alan Shoe for her, as well as set the table for dinner for Lucian's family. "There are eight of us, counting my parents. That's a lot to throw at someone so close to dinner. And it's also not necessary."

"If you think I'm going to be mated to you without meeting the people who raised you, you're dumber than Astrid. And I have a feeling that you're far from that. Please contact the rest of your family, and we'll see where this leads us." He stood up and she sat up straighter on the couch. "Mr. McCray, this doesn't mean that I'm going into this willingly. Nor does it mean that I'm going into this—whatever it is— blindly. I might need you as much as you need me, but I'm not a pushover, nor am I easy."

"It never occurred to me that you were either. I do need you, more than I think you need me. And please, call me Lucian." She nodded. "For what it's worth, I think you could take them on, both of them, and come out on top with your family. I also think that they're going to get more desperate about things, though I don't know what those things are, before this is finished. Don't you?"

31

"Yes. I had to come home to be here for the will to be read. I'd already decided that I would perhaps stay. And after talking to your brother about how things are around here, I think I can do a lot of good too. But I can't if I have to forever wonder if you're going to pounce on me." He said he'd never pounce on her. "Good. One less thing I have to worry about for now."

He followed her into the kitchen and Dad stopped him. He simply said yes, she was his mate. For several minutes, Dad whooped and yelled. Lucian thought again that this was going too easy. Like usual, he was waiting for the other shoe to drop. But for now, he'd enjoy himself.

Chapter 3

Daxton waited for the other two to show up. He was glad that Demi had gotten herself someone to watch over her. And as far as he knew, there couldn't have been anyone better than Lucian McCray. The man came from a good family, and a supportive one. He had a feeling that this was more than just a bodyguard relationship too. They were a mated pair, if he didn't miss his bet.

When Astrid and Nathan showed up, he had to stifle his laughter because of the way the two were dressed. Demi had on a pair of nice dress pants and a lovely top, and her hair was pulled back into a thick braid down her back. Classy casual, he would call it.

Nathan was obviously hung over. His eyes were bloodied, and his nose was broken and had a large piece of tape over it. His clothing looked as if he'd slept in it. The shirt he was wearing was dirty with food stains, and bore the name of a well-known college. Daxton knew for a fact that Nathan hadn't even graduated from high school, much less an Ivy

League school.

Astrid had on a skirt that was much too small for her large frame. It was short too, but Daxton wasn't sure if it was short because of the mass it had to cover, or if that had been the style she'd been going for. Her boots were worn — one of the zippers had a pin on it to keep it together at the top. The blouse she had on was a belly one, which showed much more of her than any human would ever want to see. Mounds of fat, to him, were not sexy at all.

"We're gathered here today to read the last will and testament of Abrielle Morgan. Present are her children in order of birth; Astrid Morgan Chase, Nathan Morgan, and Demetrius Morgan." He smiled at them all. "Now, if you'd all give me your unopened envelopes, we can proceed."

Demi, as he knew she would, handed hers to him unopened. Nathan said that he'd forgotten his, but would bring it by some other time, and Astrid handed hers to him not only opened, but with a large coffee stain on it.

"You were to bring them today, unopened and not read. Without them, I told you that you'd forfeit some of your estate. It seems that Demi is the only one that can follow instructions." Daxton listened to the older two argue. They were being snide to Demi, but she just sat there saying nothing, and her face looked as if she were the only one in the room with him. "Demi, there is something for you at the end of this. I'd like to see you right after, if you'd not mind."

"All right. But I don't care about it...whatever it is, I just don't care." He'd known she'd say that as well. He had known the family for a long time and knew the troubles that had kept the younger one in the hospital a great deal. Also, he knew that she'd left home very young and hadn't ever returned, except for her grandma's funeral. "Can we get this going before they kill each other?"

Daxton nodded and went over the terms of the will — who had written it, the day that it had been sealed, and who had witnessed it. Demi was surprised that her grandma had been one of the ones who had signed off on it. And when Lucian put his hand on her shoulder, she took it like a lifeline.

"Can we please get to the good stuff? Like what did she leave us? I'm not sure why this had to be done, a will and all, but it's messing up my daily routine. I was to have my nails done today." No one pointed out that her nails, as she called them, were bitten down to the quick. But that was Astrid, a woman who made appearances of having more than she ever would. "Get on with it."

"All right. To Astrid, I leave nothing. She has been a burden on me for the last twenty years. I never realized it before, but since you were ten years old, I have done nothing but pick up one mess after the next that you got —"

"Hold on a damned minute here. What does that mean, she isn't leaving me anything? You must have read the name wrong. Start again, and this time get it right." Daxton had expected this and repeated it, saying the name and spelling it out for her. "No. I don't understand. There must be something wrong with this thing. What does Nathan get? Is he supposed to get something that he's to share with me? That's it, right?"

"If you'd let me finish, then we can get you to your appointments. And I have read it correctly. Your mother goes on to say that she's paid for six of your divorces, medical procedures for unwanted children, as well as paid for you to have dental work done when one of your ex-husbands bashed your teeth out." Astrid stood up and Daxton did as well. "Sit down."

Not only did she sit, but she looked confused about it. Daxton was a very old vampire and could have made her climb the walls should he have wanted. But this had to be done and done today. The deadline was coming up.

"I want you to get to my part in this." Nathan smirked at his sister. "Go on, tell me what I'm going to get, and then I can go to the house and have the entire thing redone to suit me. Astrid can stay with me if she pays rent, but it'll all be mine."

"To my son, Nathan. I leave nothing as well." Nathan stood up but sat down when Daxton only stared at him. "I have paid more than a mother should for his fights, his drunken behavior, as well as the women that he thought to knock around. There were grandchildren that didn't make it into this world that I will never see, never hold. All because of your temper and ill mannerisms."

They both looked at Demi when he did. Nothing could have made him happier than reading the next part to the rest of them. He'd been keeping up with Demi throughout her years and knew that the things coming to her wouldn't even be a drop in the ocean for what she had currently. But it was amends being made — a gesture from a mother to a daughter.

"I leave to my daughter, Demetrius Morgan, everything that I have. The house, which you have been paying on to keep it livable, was signed over to you weeks ago." Daxton looked at Demi. "This was before I found you, so it has been about four months now. There is more, but there is a portion that is only for your ears."

"All right. And how did she know that the house had been paid off and the taxes caught up?" Daxton said it had been her grandmother. "I see. She told her for what reason, do you know?"

"Yes. But again, that is a portion of the will that is for your ears only." Demi looked at Lucian, and then at her brother and sister. The resemblance had been there, a long time ago. But age, drinking, and eating things that were not good for either of them had taken their toll on them. "Shall I continue?"

"This is an outrage. What do you mean she gets everything? She didn't even live there with us all this time. I will contest this will. See if I don't." Nathan looked as if he was going to hurt someone before he sat down. Daxton only laid the file that he'd been putting together for some time now in front of Nathan—the doctor bills, cars crashed, drinking rows that had cost a fortune to have repairs made. Nathan turned his nose up at it. "Mother was supposed to take care of us. We were her children, for Christ's sake. Whatever she paid, it was her duty as our mother to make sure that we didn't get into trouble."

"And what about me, Nathan?" He only waved Demi off when she spoke. "What about my being taken care of? My needs? There wasn't anyone there for me when you knocked the shit out of me and sent me to the hospital. Or when you and Astrid stole all my money that I made."

"What were you going to do with it? Save it? Christ, Demi, money is made to have fun with. At least until you're too old. Saving for a rainy day? What did it get you?" Daxton leaned back, hoping she'd tell him just what she'd gotten. "Nothing, I tell you. A falling down house that you no more deserve than that low life behind you."

"Low life? He has more integrity than ten men like you. He works hard and takes care of his parents, not the other way around. And you ask what I have? What I got out of saving my money? Here, let me tell you." She pulled out her phone and opened it. "At this moment I have three bank accounts totaling about seventy million dollars. I have nine profitable businesses that are making more money than you've been able to toss away in your lifetime. I have ten homes all over the world. Money in banks that is earning interest for me. I could buy and sell you a million times over, and not even worry about where my next meal was coming from. You ask why I should get everything? I'll tell you. Had it not been for me, you and your sister would have been tossed out on your broke asses a very long time ago. And despite the way I was treated, I still to this day take care that you have a roof over your fucking heads and food on the table, you fat lazy piece of fucking shit."

When Demi was finished, she stood up. Anger was like a blanket over her, and when Lucian reached for her, Daxton was glad to see her go into his arms where she belonged. This, he knew, was going to be a match for the ages. They needed each other and would go a long way in making things right for themselves.

"If you're so fucking rich, which I don't believe for a minute, then why the fuck are you getting everything that we should have?" Lucian asked Astrid if she'd been paying attention to her sister. "Big words, but no proof. If you have all this, I want you to sign Mom's house over to me and keep taking care of us. It's the least you can do, because you took all of our inheritance from us."

Daxton looked up Demi's name on the computer. He was impressed with the woman and turned his computer to her sister. Right there, it spoke of her being the richest woman on the planet. That her ability to turn a nickel into a million was renowned. Both Nathan and Astrid stopped bickering to look at the article that stated that she was one of the most sought-after women in the world, and that she was as difficult to find as a needle in a haystack.

He knew what the article had said. That she was a recluse, that she didn't grant interviews, and she didn't go out to dinner unless it was a function. And even then, no one knew her. There were no pictures of her, nothing to say that she worked hard despite having all the money she'd ever need. He looked up when Lucian stood in front of his desk.

"I'll bring her back later today. She's upset." Daxton looked at Demi and could see that if she was upset, which he'd be as well, she didn't look it. "I'll let you know when, all right?"

"Yes, of course. Thank you, Lucian. And congratulations." The younger man only glanced at the computer, and Daxton knew just where his mind was going. "It won't matter a hill of beans to her. You can make her happy, that's all that will matter in the end."

"If you say so. I had no idea." Daxton nodded. "I'll call you later and set up a time for her to come back."

After they left, Nathan and Astrid started arguing again. They wanted to know how they could go about having the will changed, to make it so that they even got a portion of Demi's money.

"We can sue her, can't we? I mean, she didn't even share her money with us all these years. We should have been getting a check monthly from her." Daxton asked Nathan why he thought that. "I don't know. Because we didn't kill her off when she was a kid? I mean, it was tempting. And I just don't understand why Mom would have left her everything. The house should have been ours, not hers. It's not like she needs it or anything. She said that Grandma, the old bitch, left her her home as well. That really isn't fair, do you think?"

"What I think is that this meeting is over." Daxton stood up while the other two looked at him like they were ready to pounce. "I'd like to give the two of you a bit of advice. First and foremost, I'd leave Demi alone. She's happy now and will be for a lot longer than either of you will, but her husband to be is also a bear shifter. Not your run of the mill shifter either, but one that loves her enough to kill you without a second thought. The second thing is, I'm a vampire of considerable age and magic. You fuck with me, either of you, and it will be the last thing you ever do. Do I make myself clear?"

"Yeah, you do. But we're going to get a piece of her, even if we have to kill that man to get to her." Daxton only shook his head at Nathan. "And you are going to be looking at a way to get us a part of that money too. Do I make myself clear?"

Daxton let his beast go. That was all it took for the two of them to know that they were barking up the wrong tree. Taking them out of his offices and to the middle of a field, he stripped them both down to their skin and left them there. They'd have to figure out how to get home on their own now. And it would buy poor Demi a few days of not having them as a threat.

~*~

Lucian didn't say a word on the way home. He drove her rental like he had this morning on the way in, but he was quiet now, like he was processing the fact that she had money.

Looking at the new car lot, she asked him to pull in. Lucian did so without a word.

"This is what's going to happen. Are you listening to

40

me?" He nodded but didn't speak. Demi slapped him. "Now do I have your full attention?"

"You're very violent, aren't you? I said I was listening. What is it you need?" She told him to pay attention. "I am. Christ. Are you really that wealthy?"

"No, we are. As of nine this morning, your name is on everything that mine is on, except for this car. Which we're going to take care of right now." He was shaking his head. "Why not? Do you have something against driving a car that is younger than you are? I don't doubt that you take good care of it, but—"

"I don't want you buying me anything." He was angry, and she was getting there too. "Look, I had no idea that you had all that stuff—money, homes, and businesses. We should just call it quits. That way you can go your way, and I can go on living the way I did before. It'll be better for us both."

"I see. And the fact that you tasted my blood, that won't affect you at all." His cursing was loud and long. "I'm taking that as a yes. All right, you don't want a new car. Tough shit. I need you to drive me around, and if my family comes after me while I'm out and about, I'd like to know that you can get to me without having to baby talk your truck into starting. Gannon told me that you have to do that on cold mornings, as well as warm ones."

"That's no reason for you to buy me a fucking car." She looked out the window and thought about his anger. Getting out, she went to the first car she saw and wondered if he'd fit under the steering wheel. "What do you think you're doing? I told you I don't want a car."

"Well goody for you. I hate paying rent on something that isn't necessary. I need one even if you're being too childish to

41

understand that you need one as well." She moved to where the nice SUVs were. She had one at home she was going to have to sell off, she realized. "I have to have the one at home sold or brought here. Do you think that your parents would want it? It's only a couple of months old."

"Probably. The one that they're driving now is— You're not paying attention to me. And I want you to look at me while I talk." She turned and glared nastily at him, and he flushed brightly. "Okay, that wasn't called for. I'm sorry. Again. But we don't need you buying us a car. None of us do."

"I'd like one." They both turned and looked at Josiah. She'd forgotten that he told her he worked here. "I get a really good discount. Are you going to buy Lucian one too?"

"He said he doesn't need one. He's being childish." She moved around the lot with his brother. Josiah showed her the options on the car she'd been looking for, and things that she could get on one too. "I'd like to get this one. How many colors does it come in?"

"Seven. One for each of us." She nodded. "No, I was joking. You aren't going to buy me a car, Demi. I can't afford to pay you back, and I'm certainly not going to be beholden to you."

"We're family, correct?" Josiah nodded; he looked at his brother, then back at her. "Family helps family, from what I understand. Since your pigheaded brother won't take a car to rescue me when I need him, then perhaps I can convince you to do it. I will need you to make sure that I'm—"

"I'll take a car." She smiled at Lucian. "You're not a nice person. I don't like being blackmailed."

"I don't like resorting to it either, but you literally left me no choice." He nodded. "What color do you want? I want the

42

dark blue one. But if you'd rather have it, then I can take the red one."

"I'd rather have the blue one." She nodded and turned to Josiah. "How many do you plan on buying today? If you're going to do this, then I'd like some input."

"Good. I want you to have input. I just realized today when we were in the attorney's office that I've been alone for so long that I want to interact with others. And when you took my hand, offering me comfort, I knew then that I needed you much more than you do me." She walked away and looked at the other cars or tried to. Her eyes were filled with tears. He'd cheapened the outing. Not that it was his fault, not totally, but she'd wanted to do something nice, and he'd made her feel shitty.

"Demi?" She turned and looked at Lucian, not even bothering with wiping away the tears. "I'm so very sorry. I'm an ass, and worse than that, I made you hurt. I want you to know that I'm not normally so...I guess you could call it so selfish. And I was. Not allowing you to do something nice for me, for my family, was a selfish act, and I am profoundly sorry."

"Thank you. But let me ask you this. Would you have done the same thing for me if things were reversed? Bought me a car and one for my family when you knew that they were in desperate need of one?" He nodded. "So, it's not the money. It's because as a female, I shouldn't be allowed to do something."

"Pretty much. As I said, I was selfish. And I'd like nothing better than for you to buy me a car. All of us, if you'd like to. But nothing too extravagant. You didn't get all this wealth from buying willy nilly, did you?" She laughed when he did.

43

"Again, baby, I'm so sorry. I'll learn to keep my mouth shut."

"Yeah, well, I'll believe that when it happens."

They walked around the lot for over an hour. They had a good time, and when he suggested they get dinner when they were finished, she said that was a good idea. Going into the storeroom, Demi made her way to Josiah's desk and sat down.

"I can't sell to you." She asked him why not. "You're my sister-in-law. And that is against the rules."

"But I'm not your sister-in-law. No one has even asked me to be a part of this family. You'll sell to me or I take my business elsewhere. Tell your boss that." He grinned at her and she winked. "If you'd like, I will tell him the same thing. I'm here to do business, and if he's not willing to accommodate me, then he's going to be shit out of luck."

Josiah went to get his boss. When Mr. Caplin was sitting at Josiah's desk, she asked him what he was doing. He told her that he was going to write up the sale.

"Will he get the credit for it?" Mr. Caplin looked at Josiah then at her, shaking his head. "I see. So, you'd take full credit for him making a nice sale."

"That's the way we've done things here for a long time, Ms.... I don't think I caught your name." She told him. "Well, Ms. Morgan, it would seem impartial of the company to let him take credit for a sale to his family. The commissions aren't the big issues here, but—"

"Not to you perhaps." She stood up and so did Lucian. He was grinning from ear to ear, and she didn't have any idea why. "Will you excuse me just one moment?"

Mr. Caplin just leaned back in his chair. He had a smile on his face that made her think that he thought he'd won.

Demi was a good business person, and she hadn't gotten that way by taking shit from people who thought they were smarter than her. Pulling out her phone, she called Mr. Lesley of Lesley Motors, where they were.

"Hello, Jamie, how are you and your lovely family?" He told her that all was fine, and he'd been thinking about her. "Oh, me too. We have to get together soon. I have some ideas for you on that new place you're thinking of opening. But the reason I've called you. I'm trying to buy some cars, and your dealership has this ridiculous rule about someone selling them to me. We're not family, but he's using that as a rule to take the commissions for himself."

"Let me guess. The Ohio one near where your grandma lived." She said that was the one. "I have had more complaints about him in the last six months than I have all of the others together. How many were you thinking of buying, Demi?" She told him at least ten. "Yes, well, I bet he didn't mention the bulk discount either."

"We didn't get that far. I don't want to cause you any trouble, Jamie, but I do want this to be done by the man who took us around. And yes, he is related to the man I'm seeing, but that isn't any reason for him to lose the commission on the sale, do you think?" He said that Caplin had made that rule up on his own. "I see. No, actually, I don't. How long as he been doing this?"

"For far too long. That man that took you around, you think he'd be able to take over the job? With you in his corner, I don't see a problem with it if you don't." She said that she would guide him. "Well, that's about as good as it gets where I'm concerned. Please put the unemployed jackass on the phone for me, dear. And we really do need to get together.

45

Very soon. I have an idea that you're going to suggest that I build there."

Demi handed the phone to Mr. Caplin and pulled Josiah to the side. As Caplin talked—begging, it sounded like to her—she told Josiah that he was going to be the new manager. He, of course, had to have a seat—on the floor.

By the time Mr. Caplin was being escorted out, she had Josiah believing that he could run a multimillion-dollar business. She, of course, didn't mention that part, but let him believe what he wanted for now. As her sales were written up, he kept asking her if she was kidding him.

"Two things that I never kid about, Josiah—money and love. Ever. You will do a bang-up job here, and I have all the faith in the world in you. So does Mr. Lesley. And if you and I play our cards right, we can talk him into bringing his plant here and hiring a great many people."

"That would be wonderful for the town. You're really making a difference, Demi. And I'm thrilled shitless that you're going to be Lucian's mate." She just looked at the man in question. "You might even make him realize that it's nice being rich. I don't know, but you just might."

They bought ten of the SUV's. Two were on the lot, which she and Lucian were going to take, and Josiah made arrangements with another lot to have ten more brought here. He figured that if people were going to have jobs, they would want new cars too. Demi thought that Josiah was going to be good at his new job. Now all she had to do was convince Lucian that having money wasn't all that bad.

Chapter 4

Lucian sat at the desk in the biggest house he'd ever been in. Taking in the room, he tried to wrap his mind around what Mr. Shoe had just told him—or had been trying to tell him. Not only was Demi wealthy, but she had contacts all over the world that she could call on to make things happen.

"Are you all right?" He nodded at Alan, what he'd been asked to call his new attorney, then shook his head. "I know just how you feel. When she hired me, I was nothing at all. An ex-con that was as down on his luck as anyone could be. Hell, I was living in a box behind a department store."

"But you're an attorney." He nodded and sat down across from him. "She helped you out? By sending you to college?"

"Not hardly. As a matter of fact, I was already an attorney. But I lost my wife and daughter in a car accident. A drunk ran a light and hit our car dead on. Killed my little girl instantly, and my wife died a few days later. I was injured, but nothing I couldn't have come back from. So, when I met Demi, she literally picked me up, shook the shit out of me, and told me to get my act together. It took me three months to dry out. Yes, I'd taken to drinking my sorrow away. I got help in the form of a doctor, got my licenses to practice again, and have been sober and working since. If she sees something in you, you can bet that she'll make you see it too in no time."

"I've noticed that. My brother, he was a salesman at a shitty car dealership, and now he's running the place. She made a single phone call to make that happen. And I'm driving a brand-new car, something that I've never had before, and there is one for each of my brothers and my parents. I'm a little overwhelmed right now." Alan said that he would get used to it. "You think? I don't. I'm terrified that she is going to wake up and realize that we're not suited. The other shoe, no pun intended, is always dropping on the wrong side of the bed for me."

"I'd get over that if I were you. If the shoe were going to drop with her, she'd have hit you in the head with it right from the start. Demi is smart. She's a good woman, too. But she is also stressed out, all the time. She needs someone to tell her to slow down. I'd not do it in that tone or words, but she needs to enjoy her life before it causes herself to have a heart attack. And she has had some scares, too." Lucian asked him when that had happened. "A few years ago. She'd been trying to buy out a company that was failing. Like, failing so badly the owner wasn't going to be able to hit his next payroll. But he finally got a clue, did what she told him, borrowed enough from her to hit the next three payrolls, and the man is sailing on easy street now. So, your brother had better listen to Mr. Lesley. He knows she isn't wrong about much."

"That's why he was so willing to listen to her when she told him to hire Josiah." Alan nodded. "She's really as wealthy as she told us in the attorney's office that day."

"I'd say she glossed over a few things. Quite a bit, if I know her. She might have said something like a few million?" Lucian told him what she'd said about the homes, banks, and businesses. "Nah, that's not even close." Lucian let out a long breath. "She is a multibillionaire; owns about fifty profit making companies, as well as hundreds of homes that she mostly rents out to people who've done something nice for her, and a few dozen warehouses that simply hold things so that when there is a disaster someplace, she can send water and supplies at a moment's notice."

"Christ." Alan laughed and told him that he was also the owner, as well as a multibillionaire. "I don't think I like you overly much right now."

"Yes, you do. And do you want to know why? I'm here for you at any time you get overwhelmed, overheated, or need advice. She saved my life, and I want to help you along this path so that you can be as successful as she is. And you will be. You just have to get used to saying you can instead of you can't. All right?" Lucian thanked him. "You might not want to do that just yet. You're going to have to help me put money in the accounts of your family members, and then you're going to tell them."

No, Lucian thought, he did not like this guy. But he realized when they hacked into the accounts that his family members were much worse off than he thought they were. His parents were getting a check each month and his dad worked a fulltime job, but they only had twenty-three cents in their account, and Lucian knew for a fact that Dad didn't get paid for a few more days.

The other accounts weren't much better. Josiah was the

only one that had more than twenty dollars in his account, and it wasn't much more than fifty dollars. Lucian's account had been closed and his information added to Demi's account. He was also given credit cards with his name on them, as well as a list of all the stores that he would have an account at. When they were finished, Lucian felt drained. It was hard for him to know that his family was far more in the hole than he'd ever imagined.

"You did well." Lucian told Alan that he had to tell his family yet. "It'll be hard on them. I've noticed that you have a very proud family. But think of it this way, Lucian—you've opened the door for them to have better lives too. You could have told me no and I would have abided by your wishes. But you didn't, not even balking when you saw how much we were to put into each account."

"My mother is going to have a brick. And my dad will try and make me take it all back. I have to think of something to tell them so that they'll be able to live with this and still be able to show their faces to Demi. They'll think that she'll think less of them." Alan said Demi would never do that. "You know that, and I do as well. But they're going to have a hard time with it. I do have a favor to ask of you. You can tell me no or have me ask Demi if you need to. But I'd like to find a home for my parents that isn't quite as run down."

"That's an excellent idea. And as a matter of fact, there is a home just down the road from yours and Demi's home. It's very nice, one floor, though I don't think they'd have a problem with stairs for a long while yet. It has four or five bedrooms for the grandkids when they start coming along, as well as a pool that's heated." Lucian asked if he had to talk to Demi first. "You can if you wish, but she'll just tell you that it's your money as well. She has told me that you speaking or requesting anything is the same as it coming from her. And she has mentioned that they need something that will not need pans to keep the water out of."

"I hadn't noticed that until recently. They've been making do for a while now, I think." Alan nodded. "You've done your homework on my family. Is there anything else that I should know about them? Something that I can upgrade, fix, or improve for them, to make their lives better?"

Instead of answering him, Alan handed him a file. He was almost afraid to open it, fearful that he'd find that his family was on the verge of going to jail or something. But the list, in order of names, wasn't that bad. The money that they'd put in their accounts would take care of most of it. There were also a few things that he could take care of easily by just having them buy a home.

Pierce didn't have a furnace at the moment and hadn't had one in about two years. Keeping his house warm by heaters was sucking him dry with electric bills being high. He'd also been walking to work as a cashier at the local grocery store, winter or summer, because his car would sometimes start, but mostly didn't.

Ian had a job, but he was overqualified for it. While none of them had gone to an Ivy League college, they had gone to the local college when they could afford it. Ian had a degree in computer science.

Madden had a job as well—he worked the lines at a distribution center that, like the one Lucian had worked for, was probably going to close up. There weren't a lot of people around that could get back and forth to the place. It was nearly sixty miles away, too far for most people to travel.

Gannon worked at the mall, and lately it had taken a hit from all the unemployment going on. Gannon was just saying the other night that his job as a photographer was probably going to end soon, as no one could afford to have pictures taken by a professional. It looked as if all his family would be hurting sooner than he thought.

After Alan left him, showing him how to find the information that he wanted on the computer, Lucian sat there for another two hours. It wasn't until his dad came in the room with him, clearing his throat, that he realized how much he had to learn about being a wealthy man.

"You did something today that I'm none too happy with you about." He asked him if it was the money. "You know good and well that it is. What right do you have to go about snooping around in mine and your mom's account like that? You think you need to save us because you've gotten a little pocket change? I don't want it. You take it back."

"When I became Demi's mate, she put me on all her accounts. And when I say all, I mean all. She saved me, with her multibillion-dollar enterprises." His dad leaned back in the chair, his face pale with shock. "Yes, that's the way I felt too. And since she has helped me, I wanted — no, that's not right. I needed to save you all as well. Dad, we will never miss the money. And from what Alan told me, she makes more than I put into your account every day in investments, interest, and rent from her other homes."

"She's that wealthy?" Lucian told him that they both were. She had given him access to all that she had. "That's a good girl you have there, Lucian. But I still don't like that you've done this. You should — I was going to say save for a rainy day, but I have to tell you, it's been pouring buckets at our home."

Dad wiped his face. The tears were there, sliding down his weathered cheeks. Lucian got up and went to his father and hugged him. He could feel Dad's body shaking with his emotions as he sobbed on his chest. Lucian felt his own eyes fill with tears.

"Your mom, she's fit to be tied, I tell you. But she sure is loving that new car. I have to admit, it is nice having one that turns over every time you turn the key." They both laughed, and Dad looked up at him as he continued. "Lucian, you helping your brothers out too?"

"I am—I have. They've been given enough to do whatever they wish. But I do have one more thing to talk over with you. A new house." Dad started to speak, but Lucian asked him to wait. "The house you're in is older than you are. It's not fit to even be fixed. And the house that I'm thinking about, it's within walking distance from here. You could just pop over whenever you want, and you'd be close enough to babysit for us."

"You're going to have babies for me?" He smiled. "That didn't come out right, but you understand me. To have a grandchild sure would make it nice. And that old house that we live in…. I have to tell you, son. The thought of having a little one in that house would scare me, the amount of things wrong with it. The other day your mom nearly broke her leg falling through the floor in the kitchen. I wish I could have done something then."

"Like I said, Dad, it's not worth fixing anymore. So, all right. You go with me to look the house over, and we'll see if Mom will like it better than where she is." Dad told him she'd live in a dog house if the floors were secure. "I think we can do a little better than that. And having you close is about all a son can ask for, I think."

"Yes, that and the love of a good woman. You tell her that you love her yet?" He said that he'd not thought of it. "Well, I know you've not mated or anything. You giving me and your mom grandchildren will be easier if you do. I think you should get on that right away. Don't push her — I think she'd hurt you if you did — but sooner would be good."

They got into Dad's car and drove to the address where the house was. Even from the driveway, he knew that Mom would flip out over it. It was a one story, yes, but it was a huge flipping home. And Dad loved it so much, he danced in the driveway even before they saw the inside of it. Yes, Lucian thought, having funds sure made him feel better than he had in a while.

~*~

Demi looked over the report that she had from the restaurant. All the cameras were installed, as well as the rooftop ones that not only looked over the parking lot, but the receiving door as well. Just as she was trying to figure out the angle of the camera in the kitchen, Gannon walked in. She could tell immediately he was pissed.

"What do you know about cameras, other than they can take pictures?" He paused in his anger long enough to look at her, confused. "You know what I mean. Like, I have several cameras in this restaurant that I own, and all I can see right now is the kitchen stove. That's not what I want to look at."

"Do you have a remote camera? I guess you do. What I meant was, do you have one that will allow you to change the view?" She knew that she did but told him that she didn't know. "Would you mind if I had a look to see?"

"No, please do." She got up from her desk and let him sit at it. She had several monitors on the wall next to her desk, each of them to a different place that she owned. And they would change to different places at a touch of a button. "I have a lot of things going out the door there, and I want to keep an eye on the storage locker. It's not a freezer, but it gets pretty cold. That's why I was told that they couldn't put a camera in there. It would frost up or steam up if the door was open too often."

"Not necessarily. There are cameras that you can have put in that are made for just that." He glanced at her as he played with the cameras. "I was going to ask if you could afford it, but I'm willing to bet you could afford the company that makes them. This does not lessen the fact that I'm pissed off about the money you put in my account."

"Get over it, jackass. We put money in all the accounts, including your mom and dad's. The camera needs to show me who is taking what out of the storage unit. And I already have one at the back loading door. I need to make sure who is doing it, and how much each person is taking before I can have the police go in." He asked her what they were taking just as he lined the camera up to where she wanted. In less time too. Demi told him. "Profitable. Nothing that can be traced because of no numbers on it. No fingerprints, and the best part of stealing something like that is, you could have one hell of a party and eat up all the theft."

"What did you just say?" Gannon turned and looked at her. His face looking like he was in trouble. "My chef is having this grand summer party. He even invited me. I was told that he'd had a big windfall at the races and that he was paying for it from that. Christ, you think he was inviting me to rub it in my face that he was getting away with it?"

"I wouldn't know for sure, but if that's the first thought that comes to your mind, then yes, I'd say that was what he was doing." She swayed on her feet, and he turned from the computer to help her to a chair. "If you pass out on me, Lucian is going to come here with his great big bear and I'm going to be toast. Are you all right?"

"You McCray men, you're all charmers, aren't you? Yes, I'm fine." She looked at the computer and then back at him. "What can I do to make sure that these stay on this area all the time? I'm sure there is some sort of locking app for it, correct?"

"Yes." He locked it in place. "I'm assuming that you put these in at some time so no one knows about them. And that you have one on the front door as well."

"Why the front door?" He told her that they could just as easily take it out that way. "Okay, I've decided that you're working for me. You have a mind more devious than mine. The job you have now, you're much too overqualified for it if you have a handle on how to work this stuff."

"Most of the time I have nothing to do, so I utilize the computer at work. And since they were willing to pay for me to take some classes, just to keep up on the latest photo trends, I added in a few extra ones that would help me should the industry take a leap from the thirty-five millimeter that I'm currently using."

"You do know that we've all gone to digital, don't you?" He just grinned — the charming part of the McCray men. "All right. That job you have, it's not going to be around much longer anyway, right?"

"No. I got word today that the mall has been bought and is being torn down for something else." She smiled at him.

"You didn't."

"I did. And I got it for a song compared to what I'm going to sell it for once the building is gone. How about you come and work for me, Gannon? I'll put in the industry that is going to bring about seven hundred jobs to this area, and we'll be even." He asked her about the money in his account. "Really? You were seconds away, from what I heard, from losing your ass because you were going to bounce several checks. And not because of me. The company that you worked for, they closed up shop and skipped out on covering payroll. It's only two people, but that still doesn't make it right."

"No, it— Lucian wants to talk to you. He said that he exchanged blood with you, but he didn't want to freak you out if he spoke to you. Something about a house and the bank." She asked if he was in trouble. "I believe so. You might want to go to your neighbor's house—the one that my dad is trying to buy. And my mom is there too. She is fit to be tied."

She'd never known what that meant literally, but she knew that she was pissed. About what Demi didn't know, but she made her way to the house next door with Gannon. In order to calm her mind enough to think, she told him what she'd pay him, his perks, and what she'd make sure he had. Lucian spoke to her before she saw the police and house.

Don't get mad at me. She told him she wasn't. *Okay, but I was trying to negotiate a better price on this house. It's been on the market for about four years, I kid you not. But Mom and Dad decided that they want it for our children to be safe, and the banker is giving us a hard time. About money.*

Okay, I'm nearly there. But answer me this. Do we have children? He laughed. *What sort of trouble are you in with the police?*

The banker called them. He has told them, and anyone that will listen, that we cannot afford this home, and that we're taking up his time and that of the realtor. I haven't any idea why that was warrant enough to call the police, but they're here and as confused as I am.

She could see the house now, and the two cruisers. Gannon was laughing, and she asked him what was going on.

"Mom is ready to shift and show the banker what it means to call her a deadbeat. And Dad is— What did I say now?" She asked him if the banker had really called Cindy a deadbeat. "Yes, but it's not the first time he's done that. The fact that we were, until this morning, makes him think that it's his right to do so."

"That isn't going to happen again." She made her way over the falling down fence that separated the two properties, and decided to have a nice path put in, one that had plants and stuff along the way so a child.... Shaking her head, she smiled at the first officer that she came to. "My name is Demetrius Morgan."

"Yes, ma'am, we know who you are. I'm glad to see you've come back home. Sure was a shame about your grandma." She thanked him. "This here, I don't know what's going on, but that banker, Mr. Mills, has a burr up his butt about something."

"What banking branch is it?" Mr. Mills came to her and screamed at her, demanding for her to tell him what her part was in this. Obviously, he wasn't so happy to see her back, if he knew her at all. As she was putting up her hand to shut him up, the officer answered her. Mills tried his bullying tactic again, and she turned to him. "You fucking prick, get out of my face before I rearrange yours for you. Now back the fuck off and shut that mouth of yours before someone shuts it for you."

No one said a word as she moved away, taking out her phone. She called the branch in town to ask for the corporate number. Within ten minutes of being switched around, she finally had the president of the National Savings.

"This is Demi Morgan. My grandmother was Milly Morgan." The president, James Stricker, laughed and said that he had known her well. "Yes, well, you can bet that I'm not much different than she was. This manager you have here, Mr. Mills, he's a fucking prick. And he's embarrassed me in front of my future in-laws, too, who are trying to buy a home next to where Grandma lived."

"And what are his accusations?" She told him what he'd said to Mrs. McCray, and that it had been mentioned to her that this was an ongoing insult to the family. Then she told him how as far as she knew, all their accounts were up to date. "Yes, I can see that they are. Since early this morning. And his beef with them? Better yet, may I speak to Mrs. McCray? I'd like to talk to her for a few moments, if you don't mind."

"If she'll talk to you. She's pretty pissed off at having the cops called on her." He asked if they were still there. "Yes. And imagine my surprise when he got all up in my Kool-Aid too. I'm telling you right now, I can pull all my accounts out of your bank, and find—"

"No, no. I'm sure we can resolve this. Just allow me to speak to Mrs. McCray, please."

She called Cindy over, and Demi told her to be just as pissed with him as she'd been with Mills.

"Oh, you have no worries on that one, my dear." She took the phone. "Listen to me, you overpaid jack ass. I'm not accustomed to being treated this way on—"

Lucian walked up to Demi just as she turned away from Cindy. She had it handled. Lucian, however, looked like a little boy caught looking at girly magazines in the bathroom.

"I'm so sorry." She asked him for what. "This. This is a mess. And I was showing off to my dad on how I could just call up the bank and get him a home. I should have cleared it with you."

"Why?" He said it was her money. "It's our money. And if you think I'm going to have time to stop and approve every purchase you want to make, then you're off your noodle. The reason I gave you access to everything is because I want you to feel like it's all yours as well. As for buying your parents a home, wonderful. It'll be really nice having them so close. And showing off is an amazing feeling. It's not you that caused this, Lucian, it's that jackass banker. But I don't think he's going to be employed much longer. That's who your mom is talking to, his boss. The president of the company."

"Wow, you do have contacts in high places, don't you?" He pulled her to him and kissed her forehead. "I'd like to take you someplace, strip you down to nothing, and make love to you for the next century. I don't think that'll be enough time, but it would be a start."

"I'd like that as well." He looked down at her. "Well, we have been living in the same house for the past week. I'd like to have you in my bed as well."

Before they could make their way back home, Cindy handed her back the phone. She had a self-satisfied look on her face as she walked to her husband. Things, she knew, were about to get funny. Mills's phone was ringing even as he was demanding that the McCrays be arrested for trespassing. This would be over soon. And they could get on to more...

personal things.

Chapter 5

Cindy walked around the kitchen again. It was hers, her domain, and she was excited to know that she could cook up a huge meal and have enough room to put everything—a dining room that would hold them all, and bedrooms so that grandchildren would be able to come and spend the night. Running her hand over the counter, she looked over at her husband of thirty-seven years.

"He just gave it to us." She nodded. "I don't know how a bank can afford to do something like that. We was going to buy it. Did he know that?"

"Yes, he did. And I told him that, several times. But he said in order to make up for all the years of putting up with Mr. Mills, we deserved something. Profound, I think he called it. Oh, Alden, isn't it wonderful? And Lucian and Demi are going to help us fill it up."

"Yes, we will be needing some furniture." She smacked him on the shoulder. "I knew what you meant, honey. I did. And I can't wait for a little grandchild myself. Hell, honey, I'd be happy with him being the only one giving them to us, too."

"I would be too. We never pressured them, and I don't plan on it now. But Alden, we have a home that we can feel good about for them. A pool in the back yard. Next year I'm going to put in a garden and roses. I so want a nice bed of roses. That other home, it didn't have any room for such things." He got up and hugged her. The man could hug a person until they screamed, but this time he was gentle, his arms relaxed around her. "Alden, I have never spoken to a person like that before. But that man, Mr. Strickler, thought I'd done a wonderful job of telling him what was going on. And he told me that if I had any more trouble from the bank that I was to call him personally. Imagine that, calling a bank president personally. I've never even called a doctor personally before. Have you?"

"No, I can't say that I have. But I don't think that you having all the answers was all it was either." She said that she knew that it was because of Demi. "Yes. I heard her tell that man if he didn't fix this right now, she was going to pull all her accounts. And that's a fair amount of money too."

"She told me about the money in our account and why she'd done it. Well, why Lucian had done it. He did it for all of us. And when I get around to it, I'm going to talk to him about it too." Alden told her that he had. "And what was his reasoning for it? He'd better have a good one."

"He does. He said that Demi saved him. I wasn't sure how she'd gone about it at first, but I think it had to do with her saving his heart. Making him feel like a man. You know how it feels to go someplace and have to put it back when you want something powerfully." She nodded. "Well, I think that's what he was talking about. Not having to put back.

And I don't think he was talking about trinkets and stuff, but food and meat on the table. It's been a long while since we've been able to have a consistent amount of meat on the table."

"Yes, even though the boys have been helping us out and we live alone, it's been hard on us." She went to the living room and tried to imagine her old things in here. "We're going to let them help with the house, Alden. I know that we have a great deal of pride. I think I might have a smidge more than you, but we don't want to shame them when we have someone over."

"I doubt very much that Demi or Lucian would think a thing about what we have in our home. But I think you're right on this. We want everyone to be safe. That couch that we have that no one sits on, it's because of that spring. And you know as well as I do that all we have is hand me downs from when my parents were alive."

She nodded. Even her pots and pans, what few they had, were from them. And they'd long since run out of glass glasses and used canning jars when they were empty. Goodness gracious, it had been so long since she'd had anything new that she wanted to cry. Sitting down on the fireplace stoop, she did just that.

"Now honey, don't be crying. You know that just tears at my heart. We'll let them do whatever they want. Even buy us some shoes if you want." She glared at him. "Well, I got you to stop crying."

They were still teasing each other, the way that they were forever dealing with the pains of being broke, when someone rang the doorbell. It was a pretty sound, Cindy thought. It made her think of bells at the local church. When Alden came back, he was grinning from ear to ear.

65

"What have you done, you old fool?" Behind him were their sons, all six of them, each of them carrying a piece of furniture that still had the plastic on it. And when they just stood there, seeming to be waiting, Demi walked in behind them. She just shook her head at them.

"I think they're waiting on you to tell them where you want things, when any idiot knows that a couch and loveseat go in this room. Put the stuff down, you dummies." The furniture was put down and then rearranged the way she wanted it. Cindy looked at the new couch and Alden bouncing on it. "There's more. Perhaps it would be faster if you came out with us, Cindy, and told them which room to put it in. Then they can move it around for you when they're done. Lucian called in some of his buddies too."

"Oh my." She went to the door and stopped. There were four—four semis in front of her house. "You did this? You bought us all this?"

"No, they did. I just helped line up the trucks. I think they had a blast once they got started. Also, if you don't like something, just have them put it back on the truck and we can exchange it for something else. And there are a bunch of groceries coming too. I didn't do that either, but Lucian said if you have a new home, you need to break it in with dinner for them all. Are you up to that?"

She couldn't help it. Cindy cried. Her heart ached with the amount of love that she had for this family. Not just her boys, but her husband and Demi too. Demi had made this all possible, and words could not convey to her how it made her feel. So, Cindy did the only thing she could think of, and hugged Demi until she hugged her back. Then Cindy cried more.

It was an emotional several hours. She watched her children, all of them grown men with their own lives, and wondered how she'd managed to raise such amazing sons. They were, too. Each of them had been sending much needed money to them every week from their pay. They'd come right away if her or their father needed something done. And now, not only did Cindy have her first new home, but she had new things to surround herself in. Looking around the yard, she was as happy as she could be about that as well.

The food arrived almost the same way the furniture did. Not only was a freezer on the truck with the food, but also a new refrigerator, a stove, and a double oven that she was having installed. She was still in the kitchen when Lucian joined her. Who knew there were so many ways that a person could make a single cup of coffee or tea?

"Are you all right with this?" She nodded at her oldest son and smiled at him. "She said that you'd be. I'm telling you, Mom. I don't think I've ever been this happy in my life. And it's not the money but seeing you and Dad so giddy with this going on. And I'm so very happy we were able to get you into something newer."

"Lucian, are you in love with Demi, or her money?" He said he'd never thought about loving her. "I see. So, all this, that's all you're happy with? The things that her money can buy us all?"

"No." He cleared his throat as he spoke lower. "No, it's not that at all. I don't think I thought of the fact that I am in love with her. I…. You have to admit, it's been a whirlwind since she came along. I do love her — I know that. And before you ask, no, I've not said it to her yet. As I said, whirlwind."

"Yes, it has at that. And she is opening doors for you all as well. Did you hear about Gannon? He's going to be working for her now too. Josiah has the dealership, and I don't think he's been happier either. She's not just giving us everything, but she's making it so we can be proud of it as well." He nodded and sat down on the newly arrived chair. "She was in here earlier. I'm to have a staff. And when I explained to her that I'd done all right on my own, she said that I had, and wonderfully too. But if I hired two people, even three, that would be three more people that would have a nice income. And since this house is much larger than the one we had before, we'll need more like eight people. Then there is the yard and the trees that are out back. The pool. Demi said that for every person that any of us hire, that is one more person that has pride in himself. A meal that he can provide for a family. Shops and restaurants that will be able to hire more people because of me hiring these people. She said that paying it forward is something that she's done all her life. And it pays well when you need a helping hand."

"I'm in love with my mate." Cindy grinned at her son. "Mom, I love her. Very much, with every fiber of my being. I love her."

"Perhaps it would be better if you told her this instead of your mom. And work on some grandchildren for us, would you? Your father is about to bust, he wants one so badly." He kissed her on the cheek and started out the door. "Then I'm guessing, from the expression on your face, that we shouldn't expect you for dinner."

"Maybe not for breakfast either." Her face heated up and he came back to kiss her. Lucian was the only son that she could tease about sex and him tease her back. She had no idea why, but it was all right. "I love you too, Mom. You're simply the best there is."

"Thank you. Now go away before I have to call Demi in here and tell her what we've been talking about."

He left her then, whistling a tune. Cindy couldn't remember any time in their life that anyone in her family had ever whistled. It was a nice sound, one that she could get used to, she thought.

She started looking at the things in the pantry. It was full, and Cindy decided that she wanted to make something grand soon. A big meal, like they'd never been able to have at Thanksgiving or Christmas. Thinking about those holidays, still months away, she got excited again. Not for the food, though that was going to be wonderful, but for the things that she could get now that she had a little cash.

Cindy wouldn't be stupid with it — not her — but she would have to keep an eye on Alden. He loved the holidays; less since the boys had come along and they'd never had anything to give them much but socks and underwear. But she knew as surely as she stood there it was going to be one of the best they've ever had. She even wanted a big tree to decorate. Which reminded her that she needed some ornaments too. Oh my, this was going to be such fun. And she had to think of something very special for Demi. Without her none of them would be this happy.

~*~

They walked home, Lucian and Demi. Holding her hand in his felt right, like he'd been waiting all his life for hers to fill it. He told her that, hoping that she'd not make fun of him. But he should have known better. It wasn't her style to be cruel to people — unless they deserved it.

"When I was a little girl, I'd been kicked out of my

home. It happened a great deal, but this time I walked to my grandmas. It was quite a hike for a seven-year-old, but I made it. I showed up at her door shoeless and coatless, and she brought me inside." Lucian knew that she needed to say this, but it hurt him in ways that made his bear want to take care of. "She ran a warm bath for me, found me something of hers to wear, and fed me dinner. I will tell you that it was the first meal I'd had all weekend. But she never said a word about any of it."

"Your mother, she would do this often?" Demi nodded, and said her brother and sister as well. "I'm so sorry. I wish I had known you back then."

"You wouldn't have liked me all that much. I didn't even like me all that much. Anyway, we spent the night watching movies and eating popcorn. A girls' night, she called it." They were almost to their home, and he could see the car in front of the house. Lucian was never going to get to make love to his mate with everything going on all the time. "Then about midnight, I woke up. There wasn't anyone in my room. The doors and windows to the house were locked up tightly, as they usually were, but something woke me. As I laid there in the bed, all I could think about was what my mother had said to me. How she hated me and wished that I had died."

"I'm so sorry." She didn't say anything but looked at the car. She told him that would be Mr. Peyton again. "Yes, he called today. He said that it was imperative that he spoke to you today."

"All right. When I'm finished here, we'll talk to him, then kick him out the door. I'll race you to the bedroom. But that night, feeling dreadful about my life, I decided that I'd take my own life." He felt his heart stop beating. She hadn't succeeded but she'd tried, and that was something that scared him. "I filled the bathtub in the bathroom I had, got out a towel so no one would see my skinny naked body, and found a knife. I knew how it was to be done — to cut downward and not across. So I got into the tub and covered myself, and my grandma walked in."

Lucian didn't know the elderly woman, but he could well imagine that she'd have been upset by this, that her granddaughter wanted to die rather than face her life. While he waited on her to finish, he noticed that Daxton was on the porch, rocking in one of the large rockers.

"She said that she'd watch me die if I wanted, but that she'd just go and do the same thing when I was gone. I asked her why she'd do such a thing when there were people that needed her." He smiled; it sounded like something that his own mother would say. No yelling, just facts. "Grandma told me that life without me wouldn't be worth getting up for. There would be no more joy in her heart, because I had it all. And that my death would be the end of her anyway. I asked her why she'd say that. And she told me that it was true. That the only reason she got up in the mornings was because she knew that I might come and see her."

"What did you do then?" Demi said that she'd cried. "And your grandma, what else did she tell you? I'm sure that it was profound."

"It was. It was the best thing that anyone has ever said to me. That she loved me more than her own life." She looked at him then. "Lucian, I love you. More than I thought would be possible in my life. I want to grow old with you. Have children with you, and to become someone that she'd be very proud of."

71

"She was proud of you, honey. And Demi, I love you so much too. My heart only beats because you have filled it. I can only breathe now, smell the earth and things around it, because you awoke something in me that I never felt before. Love. You gave it to me, and I don't think that I will ever be able to show you just how much you've come to mean to me in such a short amount of time."

They kissed then, powerfully and full of the love that they'd only just discovered they had. Walking hand in hand again, Lucian knew that this distraction was a good one. Not that he knew what Peyton wanted, but right now he'd hurt Demi if he took her. His need was as powerful as he'd ever felt before, and he wanted to mark her as his own.

When they walked up onto the porch, Peyton said he was sorry for the interruption, but this was important. After he invited the man in—as a vampire he would need that—they sat at the dining room table while he pulled out a single envelope. He laughed a little, something that Lucian was sure he didn't do often.

"Your mother left instructions to give this to you alone. I don't think she would have counted Lucian as someone you would need to fear. Open it, my dear." She did, and a single lottery ticket fell out. "Your mom won—the big pot. I know that neither of you need it, the money I mean, but perhaps you can put it to good use. That was what she wanted for you, Demi. I also have a letter from her to you. I think, when your mother found out about her illness, she took a long hard look at her life up until then. When I talked to her last, she told me how horrible of a parent she'd been to all her kids. But to you she was the most cruel."

"She found out that I was paying her medical bills. That's

72

the reason that she stopped going to the hospital. And her meds too. She stopped picking them up because she knew that I'd been paying her bills." Daxton shook his head. "Then what? She could have lived had she not been such a stubborn bitch."

"The doctors found another spot, this one on her brain. They said that they couldn't operate, nor would the medications that she was currently taking help. There were other drugs, ones that would prolong her life, she told me, but only for a few weeks. Your mother was tired of trying to live." Lucian held her while she cried. He knew that she had hated her mother — he would have too — but she had still been her mother. "When she told him she was finished, she called me. And the two of us sat down and told both Astrid and Nathan."

"I'm betting that didn't go over well." He laughed and said it hadn't. "I'm sure they wanted her to take the drugs and to live."

"No. And I'm surprised that you didn't think this first. They wanted her to pretend to take the meds so that they could sell them and collect the money. They had no idea, and still don't, that you were paying for it all. They thought, as your mother had wanted, that the government was paying for it." She asked what they'd said about her dying. "Nothing. Not a single word about her health or how much longer she had, nor did they ask if she needed anything. Your grandmother showed up a couple of days later. By then, your mother was growing nearer to death all the time. Your grandmother, she passed away that evening."

Lucian didn't comment. He wasn't even sure what he could say right now. But when Demi handed him the letter, asking him to read it to her, he knew how much it was costing her to hear the things about her siblings. Things that she might well have known about her brother and sister all along. They were the worst kind of children. And he was sure they were going to pay.

Opening the letter, he looked over the two pages. The handwriting was shaky, and there were plenty of misspelled words. But he could understand what she was saying and read aloud the last words of Demi's mother.

"My darling child. I feel that I have no right whatsoever to call you that, but I have been doing some hard thinking. And none of it, no matter how I try, turns me into mother of the year. I know I cannot in any way make you believe that I am more sorry than you will ever believe. I was a horrid mother. Not just to you, but to the other two as well." Demi laid her head on the table, looking at him as he continued. "I should have been a better person. Not just a parent, mother, or friend, but a better person. But it is much too late for that now. All I can do now is ask you to forgive me enough to use the money from the lottery ticket to make a difference in a few lives. Not your own—I know that you have no more need of this money than the man on the moon does. But you will know just how to use it to make someone, anyone, feel better than I ever did you."

Lucian looked up when Moses came into the room. He had glasses of tea for him and Demi, and whiskey for Daxton. The man swallowed it straight down and laughed. Apparently, vampires didn't just need blood. Daxton told him to go on.

"Astrid has a child out there too. I know that you've hidden away a little girl from your brother. I think that is the smartest thing, among many, that you could have done.

He—I believe he has killed the women that he enjoyed. But this woman must have gotten away somehow. Thankfully. Please, I'm begging you to hide hers away too. I don't know the details on how she wasn't able to kill it as she had the others, but I'm sure that you will figure that out." Daxton stopped him from reading to say that he had all the information she needed if she'd help. Nodding, Demi took the file and laid it down beside her. Lucian read on. "I'm dying. Not that I think you'd care any—I don't deserve to have you do so. But I do care that you are and have been hurt by your family. I have spoken with your grandmother, another person that I've had to beg forgiveness from, and she assures me that you are well and doing a good job of becoming the richest woman in the world. I looked it up, Demi, and you are. I had no idea. But it's for the best that we didn't know, especially the other two. They would have easily killed you and taken all you had. I'm sorry, but we both know that to be the truth."

Demi nodded her head. "About two years ago I was in town for a meeting. I saw Nathan just as I was getting out of a cab. He didn't say a word, just came up to me, hit me in the face, then stomped on me until the police came. A few days later as I was leaving, Astrid spit in my face because I had had the nerve to press charges against her brother. Then she too beat the shit out of me." Lucian asked if he could kill them. "I love you for that, but I can't have your children if you're in prison. And they'll get what's coming to them."

Demi said it so calmly, so softly, that he thought it was the scariest thing he'd ever heard. She would get them, and they would pay. He'd bet anything that it wouldn't be with their lives, but with something that meant more to them. And he was going to have a front row seat to it.

The rest of the letter talked about things that had happened to Demi. Some of them he almost couldn't read. The others, just as bad, were things that her own mother had done to her. Abrielle Morgan had no more deserved a child like his Demi than she had a breath of fresh air. It hurt him to think this, but he was glad that she was gone. Otherwise he was sure that something would have happened to bring her between them.

The lottery ticket was discussed. She had until Monday to cash it in. If not, it would be null and void. Daxton said that he'd do it for her, to keep her name out of it, and open an account. Demi asked him if he'd be in charge of the charity that she was going to start.

"I'd be honored to do that for you, Demi. There are a great many people here in this town alone that are in need of a great deal of help. Even the elderly could use a boost." Demi told him that she would get back to him in a couple of days. In the meantime, she wanted him to contact Nathan and Astrid.

"I want to have a meeting with them. And I'd like for both you and Alan Shoe to be there as well. Of course, Lucian will be there, as will his family. I'm not stupid enough to think that I can go into this blindly." She looked at him then. "Will you marry me? As soon as a license can be secured?"

"I will. And the sooner the better." Demi kissed him. "Do I want to know what you have planned?"

"More than likely not. But I will tell you so that we can work together. In the meantime, I'm going to find this little girl. I have been keeping up on the life of Nathan's little girl. Now that we have a location for them both, we'll keep tabs on them, from a distance, and make sure that they're not mistreated nor without what they need. While they will need more than we've given them, I don't think they'll ever be mistreated." She stood up and stood there for several minutes, her mind working, he could tell. "I will have a list of things that I need from you and Alan before we do this. So, don't contact them until I have all my ducks in a neat row. In the meantime, go ahead and fix up the account for the money after you cash the lottery ticket."

When Daxton left, Lucian pulled Demi into his arms. Neither of them said anything, but it felt to him like volumes of words were being said. It was amazing to him how just the touch of someone that you loved could make you feel like you'd been together for...well, he thought, forever.

Lucian picked her up and carried her up to their room. He was going to show her how much he loved her now. Then tomorrow, or even the next day, he'd see what the plans were for the little girls. They were his nieces, he realized, and smiled all the way into the room.

Chapter 6

Lucian put her on the floor. His hands were everywhere, just touching, soothing her skin. Closing her eyes, she let him undress her. She felt cherished, treasured, and most importantly, she felt loved. And she loved him, with all that she was.

"I love the way your skin feels. So soft and toned." His tongue went along her spine, and he kissed each cheek of her ass. He massaged her thighs and dug his strong fingers into her hips, all the way, telling her what he was feeling. "You have a great many scars here."

She stiffened up and he told her to relax, he didn't care. "My brother put most of them there. And what he didn't, Astrid did. Please, I need to turn around." Lucian kissed her again, and her back felt worshiped by his mouth. When she started to turn, he put his hand on her shoulder.

"My bear, he wishes to mark you. May he? Someday he'd like to change you, so that we can roam the forest together. Play in the woods behind our home." She nodded and the hand on her shoulder shifted slowly. The great claws were the last to morph over his hand. "We won't hurt you."

Lucian's voice was rough, like making his hand into something else had shifted all of him. Not turning when he told her not to, she felt the paw as it moved down over her back, over her ass cheeks again, until it was over the worse of the scars.

The pressure wasn't too bad at first. Then as he dug deeper into her skin, she felt the pinch of his claws as they scratched over her flesh. Blood moved down her skin, hot and slick, but the pain never took her breath away, never made her want to flinch from what he was doing to her.

Then he scratched her, a long tear to her skin. She left it open as he marked her. Still there was no real pain, and it occurred to her why. He'd licked her skin. Lucian had made it so that she'd not feel the pain as badly.

Turning to look at him, she saw that he was his bear. Moving away now, she stared at him. It didn't even bother her that she was naked in front of this great big black bear. Reaching out her fingers, they shook a little, but she touched his face as he seemed to purr at her.

"You're beautiful." He leaned his head so that it was over her hand. "I've never been this close to a bear before. I mean, who would and still be alive?"

He laughed. It was dark sounding, like he was growling a little. And when he turned her around again, she felt his hot tongue over the wound that he'd created. The feeling electrified her body, made her feel as if she'd suddenly come alive. When his hand touched her shoulder, she did what he'd done, and she leaned into his human hand and told him how much she loved him.

"And I love you. You are mine, Demi. And after tonight, we'll be one forever." She said that she wanted that. "Good. The paperwork is finished. We'll marry in the morning, and you'll be my wife. But as of now, you are that already."

He turned her then, kissing her with passion that slightly overwhelmed her. Lucian must have felt it, felt her need to slow down. So, when he kissed her the second time, it was gentle, kind, but no less hungry.

When she was laying on the bed, he stood over her. His cock was hard, straining from his groin. The need to touch him, to taste, was palpable, but he warned her that she'd make him come, and he wasn't ready for that.

"But what if I am? The thought of you coming all over me has me wet, Lucian." He grinned at her. "Please. I'm so needy I could just come looking at you."

"Well, we don't want that to happen." He joined her on the bed, his big body covering hers. She spread her legs for him, wrapped her ankles around his thighs. "Christ, I love you."

He slid into her, his body filling hers so that they'd forever be one. And when he moved Demi came hard, her entire body feeling the release of it, from her hair to the tips of her toes. When he moved inside of her again, she held on. She knew that he would bring her again and again, but the one that she wanted, the release that she needed, would be epic. It would blow her head off, and she didn't care. So long as she had Lucian with her, her life would be complete until the day she died.

Lucian worked his magic over her body. Her breasts were suckled hard. He nipped at the tips, making her need double. And when he bit down on her throat, right where the pulse was pounding, she cried out again and again that she needed him.

"I want this to be good for you, love." She said that he was killing her. "Wait for it. I promise you that it will be more than you've ever had."

"No. Now. I need it now." Lucian said she was greedy. "Yes, I'm very greedy. Now, Lucian. I need it now."

With a short laugh, he pounded her. It was like she'd released a demon in him. When he bit down, this time drawing blood again, she screamed out his name as the release that she wanted took her not just under, but up and over the moon.

But he wasn't nearly finished with her. Even as she begged him to stop, her body spent, he moved again, this time gently, making passionate love to her even though her body was broken, and she couldn't move anymore.

As soon as he took her breast into his mouth, taking it all, she felt her body heat up, her pussy ready for him to take her again. Clawing at his back, her throat too raw to ask for more, he made love to her until she thought for sure he actually was trying to kill her with passion.

"When I come, and soon, I want you to bite me, Demi. Bite my throat hard enough to draw my blood." She shook her head. "You can do it. Please. I need you to bond with me, and you need to make your mark on me as well."

His lovemaking became stronger—he was taking her harder than even before. When he gave her his throat, she cried out when he bit into her. But his throat was right there, his pulse like a call for her. She sank her teeth into him and tasted the heat, the smell of the man she loved.

Drinking him down, she came three times. It wasn't until he threw back his head, his body stiff with his release, that she realized just how much she loved him. That he was her all. And when the first splash of his cum touched inside of her, Demi came hard, her body feeling torn apart then put back together over and over, until she blacked out.

Waking, the room was dark, and she looked around for Lucian. He wasn't in the bed, but his side of the big bed was still warm. When he came into the room from the hallway, she asked if everything was all right.

"Yes, great." He crawled into the bed with her after stripping off his clothing. "We might have an issue, love. I didn't realize you were in heat."

She knew what that meant, but was she ready for that? To have a baby with so much going on…. Demi looked at Lucian when he said her name. The worry was there for him. And she was sorry that she was doubting this.

"I want to have your child, Lucian. It doesn't matter when, so long as we have as many as we can." He kissed her; not hungrily, but like he was happy. And when he pulled her into his arms, she realized that he was cold. "Where have you been, in a freezer? Christ, you're like an ice cube."

"My bear, he needed to run. And it is turning a little chilly out. Hold me." She would gladly do that, forever. And as she held him and he her, she thought about a child growing inside of her. "What are you thinking about?"

"The child. I mean, is it a done deal? I know what being in heat means, but just not the mechanics of it." Laughing, Lucian told her they could do it again if she wasn't sure. "I think you might have broken me. But am I pregnant?"

"I can't tell now. In a couple of days I'll know. So will the rest of the family. I was thinking that we'd get the jump on things and tell them now. That way we get the pleasure of getting to say it first." She asked him what would happen if she wasn't pregnant. "Then we keep trying. You're going to be in heat for at least ten days. That way if this time didn't work, we'll have to keep going."

"I don't have any idea why, but I have a feeling that you know positively that I'm pregnant, and that you're just shining me on so that we will have to have sex several times a day." Lucian wiggled his brows at her. "Am I going to have your child? Tell me the truth."

"Yes, honey. You are carrying my child." She squealed and got out of bed to dance. "Had I known you'd have that reaction, I would have told you straight away. Come to bed, love. I need to hold you and our child."

It was strange, lying next to a man that she was going to marry. And to know that she was going to have his child made it all the better. They laid there until the sun came up and shone into their room and talked. There wasn't a subject that they didn't go over until he brought up the scars on her back.

"Tell me about them. My bear, he healed most of them. Until I change you, there will still be a couple of them." She shook her head, feeling her body tense up just thinking about them. "Demi, it's a given that I'm going to kill them both if you don't tell me, to calm not just me, but my bear as well. Tell me so that he can calm down enough to not take me right now and kill the fuckers."

"I don't know that you'll be any less willing to kill them if I tell you." He leaned up on his hand, his elbow close to her head. "Lucian, they were both so cruel to me. My mother, Abrielle, she wasn't much better. Are you sure that you want to hear this? I swear to you, they'll never be able to do anything like this again."

"No, they will not." There was something so final about the way he said it, as if he and his bear were making sure that she understood what was going to happen from now on. And when she looked away from him, he pulled her chin around so that she could see him. "Just start with how old you were."

"Ten. It was cold out. Christmas was just around the corner—I think a week away. I'd been sleeping outside for the last several days, and I was frozen through." He asked her why she'd not gone to her grandma's again like she had when she was seven. "I was chained up like a dog. The collar they had around me was steel. I had had a leather one but had been able to escape that one, so this one was made to last."

"I really hate those two. Go on, love. I'm here for you." She nodded and looked around the big room. "You have an entire bruin of bears at your command. Tell me, love."

"This was my grandparents' bedroom. When Grandda died, Grandma moved out of it, saying that there were too many memories in here for her to be able to sleep. So, she got me a new mattress and changed out the furniture, and it was mine when I came to stay. Nathan hated that I could be so welcome here. Astrid too, but Nathan hated that I could come here, no questions asked, and be welcomed. The day that he came outside with the whip, I knew that he meant to kill me. And as he stood over me, he said that after he was done with me, he was going to go and attack Grandma too."

"What sort of whip was it?"

Demi answered him, not really paying attention to him now. She was there again, in the yard behind the house, the dog collar around her neck as Nathan stood over her, threatening her.

85

~*~

Lucian listened to the tale. Tale really wasn't the correct word for it—more like nightmare. The things that Nathan had done to his own sister were criminal. And he would pay—either by his hand or hers, but he was going to pay.

"The day he came out, he told me he was going to teach me a lesson then kill me. He was slender then. His body hadn't yet been filled with all sorts of drink and fast food. But he was no less strong for it." Lucian held her tighter. "The whip came down on my face. I remember how it cut into my flesh. I felt the warmth of the blood and was happy for it, for just a moment. And when he ordered me to strip to my panties, I did so without hesitation, because to not do what he said would be worse. I have no idea what my mind could think of as worse than dying, but I was just a child and him nearly nineteen."

Lucian hadn't realized that there were that few years difference in their ages. He'd thought, actually, that they were much older than her instead of nine years. But Nathan had been an adult, someone that should have gone to prison, or at least jail, when he'd hurt her like that.

"He beat me with the whip. After a while, I didn't feel much of anything. My blood on my face had frozen to my cheeks and lips. The blood dripping off my back had pooled beside me and was frozen too. It was what I looked at while he hurt me—the warm blood drip drip dripping onto itself as it became a mountain of it." Lucian wanted her to stop, to not tell him anymore. But he knew that he had to hear this as much as she needed to tell him. "When he finished, I couldn't move, but not because of the pain—I didn't feel that yet—but only because I was afraid to. It wasn't until Astrid came out, throwing a bucket of scalding water on me, that I screamed. It was enough to make me faint."

"What happened when you woke up?" She turned to him, burying her face in his chest. Lucian held her tightly as her body shook with her sobs, and when she looked up at him, his heart broke for the pain he saw there. "Oh, Demi, I'm so very sorry I wasn't there to help you out of this."

"Someone called the police. My family was gone by then, and I was no longer tied to the dog house. Someone had thrown a blanket over me, I guess. When I woke up, screaming in pain when they touched me, they kept asking me who had done this to me. I didn't answer them, fearful of what would happen to me should I do that. One of the officers was in the corner of the yard throwing up."

"Were they arrested?" She shook her head. "Why not? I mean, someone had to know what they were doing to you. Whoever called the police, they had to have seen Nathan do that to you."

"Beloved pets would come up missing if they told. Windows would suddenly be shattered. Mailboxes would be broken into and checks stolen. Tires slashed. No one said a word because there were terrible consequences if they did. I was alone, except for my grandma." He held her and asked what happened to make her leave home at seventeen. "I had been working since I was old enough to pass for sixteen. Two years of hording my money and only giving them the little that I made in my checks. I wasn't waiting tables, but I did bus them. And the waitstaff would give me a portion of their tips. I could get a table cleaned and ready for another customer even before the first customer had paid and was out the door. I helped them, and they did me."

"I waited tables for a while. And even bussed a lot of them. Not an easy job, but it does make you appreciate kitchen help." She nodded and laid her head on his chest for a moment before getting up and going to the bathroom. Lucian followed her. "I take it they found your stash."

"Yes, and the fact that I was holding out on them. Holding out like I had no right to have anything for myself. It wasn't much, I know that now — only about three hundred dollars. It had taken me two years to save that, and I was going to run with it." She stepped into the shower and he sat on the counter to wait. "I came home from work and they were all waiting for me. Astrid hit me in the back of the head with what turned out to be a ball bat. Then they all pounced on me at once. I don't remember much after that. It was just a great deal of pain. Broken ribs, my left arm broken. It took me two days to crawl and limp my way to my grandma's. Had they caught me then, I'm sure that they would have killed me. Knowing where I was headed would have royally pissed them off."

He joined her when she washed her hair. Scrubbing her back, he could see that most if not all the scars were gone. And curiously enough, so was the one at her shoulder that had looked to him like a gun shot. Lucian hadn't touched her there but thought that his blood was stronger than he'd thought. The scar was nearly gone as were the rest of them.

Dressing took much longer than he was sure it should have. They touched, talked a little. Kissed each other. He told her about the scars and she just smiled at him. And when he stood behind her and put his hands on her flat belly, she leaned into him.

"I will never beat our children. I'm not saying that I won't spank them if they need it, but never more than that. I will tell them that I love them daily — hourly if they'll allow it. And they will never, for as long as I live, think that I am anything like my family." He asked if she was ready to face his. "You mean about this baby? Will they know?"

"Just that we had sex and that my bear touched you." He looked at her shoulder again and kissed it where the scar had been. It, like the others, was gone. Lucian would have to ask his parents to see if it was possible to heal someone like he had. And if he never got around to it, he was fine by that as well. "Since it's nearly lunch time now, do you want to have them all over and announce it? Also, you have news about the owner of the car dealership, don't you?"

"I do. My friend is coming to town in a couple of days to have a look at the plastic plant. Also, he wants to put in some improvements to the road that goes to the highway — widen it for trucks. They won't be coming through town, he promised me, but they will bring in more money for sure."

They were in the kitchen, getting some brunch, when the kitchen phone rang. It was nice not to have to cringe every time it rang. There were no more bill collectors calling the house to try and sue him for money he just didn't have. But the call was for him.

When he said his name, there was a pause at the other end. Lucian was ready to hang up when the man at the other end started talking. Fast, so fast that he finally had to ask him to slow down.

"I have a deal for you. If you're in the market for a new home, call me. We can fit any kind of budget and—" Lucian whistled. "That was painful, sir. Why would you do that?"

"Because I don't know who you are or how you got this

number. Lose it. Also, I'm not in the market for anything." The man started cursing. "And that will get you nowhere with me. Who the hell gave you this number?"

"Not all of us could fuck our way into someone's bed and get paid for it. I'm just trying to make a living here, buddy. If you didn't want me to call you, then why did you give your future brother-in-law your number?" The man cursed again. "Nathan said that you were a good man to cold call on. Said that you had money out the ass."

After simply hanging up on the man, he looked at Demi. She didn't look any happier, and he told her what was going on, and asked her how they would know they were together. Demi turned the newspaper around so that he could see the headlines.

"Richest woman in the world to marry a nobody?" Lucian asked her where they'd gotten that information.

"I have a good idea that it was either Nathan or Astrid. Probably both of them. And since we've not made it a secret that we're engaged or anything, it would be easy to guess. Not to mention, our license application is announced in the paper too." Lucian told her that he was sorry. "For what? It's not true, but to try and fight it, that would be just as bad. The newspaper loves a conflict."

"I guess you don't think of yourself as marrying a nobody." She shook her head and smiled at him. It was like a live wire powering him up. "I need to learn how to deal with people on that sort of level. I'm guessing that we'll get more and more calls like that from now on."

"Yes, but you handled that one just fine. We'll simply change the number in here so that Bea isn't bothered by it and go on. It's what I've had to do." She handed him the sports page as she continued talking. "I have seats at just about any sporting event you'd ever want to go to, if you're into that sort of thing. I love football and any winter sport. We could go to the Olympics sometime if you'd like too."

Lucian sat there for a few moments, and then laughed. When Demi turned to look at him, he laughed even harder. She'd just told him that they could go to the Olympics like it was nothing at all. Maybe it wasn't to her, but to him, it was a real treat. He kissed her on the mouth when he stood up.

"I love this thing that we have between us. And I have a feeling that the money is going to go a long way in opening doors that have been forever closed for myself and my family." He got down on one knee. "Demetrius Morgan McCray, will you do me the honor of becoming my wife today? Keep me in any way you see fit. Take me places that I've never been. And love me. Love me until I'm pushing up daisies with a huge smile on my face."

"I will." They kissed, and he realized that he had no ring and was just standing there when Bea handed him something. "What's that?" Demi asked.

"Your grandma's wedding ring. I have had it since she started to go downhill, lord bless her soul, and she started losing too much weight to wear it. So she had me hold it, knowing, I guess, that you'd be getting married to the best man in town and you'd need it." Lucian slipped it on Demi's finger, and wasn't surprised that it fit her. "Her old wedding dress is packed away too. You go on now, Mr. Lucian, and I'll have her ready for your wedding in a bobbing lamb's tail."

He was out the door and driving to the courthouse when he realized two things. What the hell was a bobbing lamb's tail, and how quick was that? Also, he was going to be married today. Laughing, he reached out to his family to let them know where he was and what he was doing today. Things were moving right along. After today, they'd deal with her family, and then things would be normal again.

Chapter 7

Nathan paced the room. He hated that his sister was just sitting there doing her nails like she had not a care in the world. He would love to have hit her, but that would mess up the room too badly, and they had nothing to fall back on if they had to pay for a damaged room again.

"Why is it that Mommy had a change of heart all of a sudden? I mean, she always chose us over Demi. I don't understand why she'd just up and leave us without anything, and we're the ones that was there for her all the time." Astrid just looked at him. "Okay, we might not have been there for her, but we were there all the time. But we did live there with her, and that should count for something. Demi just ran off, without a reason in the world."

He supposed that Demi might have thought she'd had a reason. Christ, he'd been beating her all her life — why did that one time have to mean she took his fun away? It just wasn't right, any of it.

"I'm having that looked into too. I think that Demi might

have had the will changed to suit herself. Did you know that she was rich?" He said that he'd not. "Yeah, me either. I was as surprised as I could have been when we looked her up for some dirt. Apparently, our dear sister has been making money hand over foot, and not sharing a dime of it with us. You'd think that by now she'd have learned her lesson on that, holding money out on us, don't you think?"

"Yes, that was some good times we had with her. And while there wasn't much money, we had fun with it. And if I think on it a little, I believe Mommy did as well. We ate well that entire day, didn't we?" Nathan sat down—pacing was wearing him out. He wore out a great deal lately. He thought of something else. "Astrid, do you think that what we heard is true? That Demi paid for the house that Mommy and us was living in?"

"I'm sure of it. I did wonder why we never got hounded by taxes like everyone else that we knew. I mean, not only that, but remember when the roof was fixed? I'm betting that Demi found out about that and had it done too. Why would she do that and not brag about it to us? I certainly would have."

Yes, Nathan would have as well. Astrid apparently finished with fucking around with her nails and stood up. She was fat too, he noticed. When the fuck had that happened? He realized that he'd missed something she said.

"I said, we have to go and see her soon. Demi owes us, and I intend to get it. The thought of her living in that big house without a care in the world just pisses me off. We can't even get back into Mommy's house now. I went by there. Did I tell you?"

"Yes, you said that all the locks had been changed and that

94

some crew was out there making repairs. They did a good job on the lawn, don't you think? I never realized that it was that bad until I saw it all fixed up." Astrid didn't say anything, but he could tell that she agreed with him. "And the new windows are nice too. I went by yesterday just to see what I could steal. That shit they have there, all that equipment? It's very heavy, isn't it?"

"I wouldn't know. I don't heft things around that I want to steal. But we do need to get on her ass about shit."

The knock at the door to the hotel they were staying in startled them both to silence. They'd been able to scrape up enough money for one night. This was their fourth day here, and every day they expected someone to come out and kick them out. But so far, they'd had room service, and the little fridge was filled every day. It had been such a treat for him to be able to drink and eat whatever he wanted from it.

Looking down at himself, he realized that he needed to stop eating everything that he wanted. He was beginning to look like a slob too. Just yesterday he'd had to leave his shirt untucked in order to cover the fact that his pants were undone. It wasn't a feeling that he liked at all.

Then there were the lesions on his leg. It was hurting all the time now, and he noticed just last week that it was starting to turn a nasty shade of purple. The bump that he'd gotten when he knocked into the chair leg was still an open wound, and seeping. It was dark pus, and that scared him a little. He'd been keeping it wrapped up until this thing started. Now all he had around it was a towel so it would not leak into his socks and shoes.

When it seemed safe for them to talk again, he went to the door and opened it up. Picking up the newspaper that was laid out every day, he laughed at the front page. It paid to have someone that you could blackmail on the newspaper. He showed it to his sister.

"Now all we have to do is wait on her to come here begging for us to put in a retraction. And that will cost them a great deal of money to maybe have us do it. Oh, and that call you made to that guy that sells land? It was brilliant. I'm sure that they're being harassed as much as possible by him." He smiled at her. Astrid was always so generous with her praise to him. "Now, let's see what else we can— What the fuck is this?"

She turned the paper toward him, and he had no idea what had pissed her off. It wasn't until she pointed to the section where arrests were made that he saw it under marriage licenses. Demi and a man by the name of Lucian McCray had filed for one. Christ, she was really getting married?

"Now what do we do? If she gets married, then she'll be giving him our money. Well, not our money, but some of it. Astrid, I don't want to live like this anymore." She read again the names of the two of them. "That's the guy we saw her with, isn't it? That family that don't have shit. She's actually marrying him?"

"Apparently so. And look at this, Nathan. Someone by the same last name has bought some property. I'm betting she's setting up his family so she doesn't have to be ashamed of them. Christ, this is really fucking up our plans. If she keeps giving it all away, what will be left for the two of us?" That didn't seem possible to him, but he wisely kept his mouth shut. If you had all the money in the world, there had to be enough for the two of them too, was his way of thinking. "Well, we're just going to have to have a conversation with

96

our little sister. It was fine that she paid for Mommy's things, but now it's our turn. And I want to know why she paid for Mommy's shit and nothing for us. That isn't right, and you know it."

"I agree. It would have been nice to have had some money to spend. I mean, I didn't get anything much for my birthday because things were so tight. And there was Mommy, lying in that hospital bed with all the good drugs in the world, and we couldn't even sell them off. That was really cruel of Demi to have someone come in and give those shots to Mommy, when we could have been selling them off. It's not like they did her any good. She died anyway, didn't she?"

"Yes, and left us all alone to deal with stuff." Again, Nathan kept his mouth shut. Mommy had paid off her funeral, or someone had, and made all the arrangements for it. The only thing they'd had to do was to get dressed and go, and even that had pissed off Astrid. There'd been no money for her hair and nails to be done, or new clothes. "I swear, Nathan, I wish every day that we'd just killed Demi off, and we'd not be in this kind of shit. We'd have all her money, the house, and even that grandmother of hers."

"If we'd killed her off, there wouldn't be any money, would there?" She growled low, and he knew that if he spoke again, it had better be something worthwhile. "Why don't we go down to the courthouse and find out when she's getting married? Could be that they're going to have this big fancy wedding, and we could go there and steal a few of the gifts. Surely she has friends that'll send her nice shit."

They got their crap together, fearful that if the room was left unattended they'd be kicked out, and their clothing, what little they had, would be taken. Nathan didn't have much.

97

When they'd gone to the will reading thing, he'd only taken his wallet. Nothing was in it, but he had figured that if there was a check or something, he'd have his identification to cash it. He'd not even figured that there would be nothing for him. His mommy had done them both terribly wrong, he thought.

Toward the end of Mommy's life, they were both wanting her to just die. Christ, she took forever, even on her last day, to just let it go. They had sat around the house, making it look like they cared that their mommy was dying, so that the attorney, who was there more than them, could see that they were good children. And that Demi was the one that hadn't even shown up for her last breath. Of course, then they'd not known that Mommy had a will and that Demi was getting it all. Had they known, Nathan was sure that he'd not have bothered putting on the act of caring. It was boring as fuck watching someone die, and he'd just as soon never have to do that shit again.

The courthouse was busy. He didn't have any idea if there was a big trial coming up. While he could read, it took him forever to try and get through a sentence. The words would give him a headache, and they'd swim around on the page so badly that he'd have to lay down after just a little bit of reading.

Astrid could read, and fast too. It sometimes made him want to hit her when she was able to zoom right through something. Usually she'd just read to him, but when she was in a snit, she'd not and just hand him the paper with a smirk on her face.

There were flowers everywhere in the big main room. He started to ask someone what was going on when he saw Demi. Christ, she looked like a pretty picture. And when she smiled, he nearly fell back from it, it was so bright. Who would have thought that something like a smile could make a person's face just shine right up?

"Hello, Nathan. You here for the wedding?" He shook his head no. Nathan had a feeling that she was the one getting married, her being all dressed up in white, but didn't say anything. "Well, I have to get going. You stay out of trouble or I will come after you."

She was gone before he could say anything, and he had planned to be pissy to her too. Maybe knock her around so that her pretty dress was all mussed up. He looked for Astrid then. Nathan was about as mad as he'd been in a long time.

"You know what I just saw?" Astrid asked if it was Demi. "Yes, and she's here in a white wedding dress. The bitch is getting married right now. Damn it all to hell and back. Why did she have to go and do a thing like this for? There will be no money left if she keeps this shit up. Just like you said. I have a mind to go and get my ball bat and use it on her again. We'll see then who she leaves things to."

In his head that had made more sense, but Astrid didn't seem to care. She was telling him now to go and find the two of them a log or something. A rock would even do. They were heading out of the big building when six men, all of them dressed up in the best-looking suits he'd ever seen, came through the door. And they had big smiles on their faces too. Made him want to knock them in the heads. He didn't, of course. They were not only bigger than him, but none of them had an ounce of fat on them either. Nathan knew his limitations, and the way to get the better of someone. Do it when they weren't looking and make it so they didn't get right back up.

They were looking for something to bash Demi's head in with when a big limo pulled up in front of the courthouse. Both of them stopped to watch. A man got out and put his hand back in to help a woman out. He didn't know who they were, but Nathan instantly hated them. Today was the end this shit of being on the receiving line for nothing. They didn't deserve this, and he was going to make sure that these people knew it, too.

He found himself a thick stick. Honestly, he was too fat to carry much more than that. When he got the money, he was going to have one of those operations where they cut off the food to your belly. Nathan was sure sick of trying to pull his belly in enough to piss, and to fit in a shower stall like a man.

They were waiting by the limo when Demi finally came out of the building. The man standing next to her was laughing, and Nathan wondered what the hell he could find so funny. Christ, he'd just married a bitch—didn't he know it?

As Demi started down the stairs, he stood up. Demi just looked at him, and then at Astrid. He had helped her find the big stone she had, but it looked stupid now that he thought about it. Neither of them were in good shape, and he could no more have run from hurting his sister than he could have walked away from a fine meal. Or a bad one, he didn't care.

"And just what is it you plan to do with that, Nathan? Astrid? Hit me? I do hope you realize that I'm no longer the child I was. I'm a grown woman who knows how to fight back." Astrid told her that she wanted her money. "What money would that be? The money that your mother had? There wasn't any. How about the estate money? Nope, not any of that either. You guys are shit out of luck, I guess."

"Demi, you're not being nice at all. You're going to get

100

yourself in a world of hurt if you don't behave and fork over some money." He looked at the men around her when she did. "We don't want to have to hurt anyone else. You just give us half of what you have, and we'll be on our way. It's the least you can do for us since you made it all without sharing when you was out of the house."

"The least I can do, Nathan, is to get into the car and go home. And that is just what I'm going to do. I don't owe you a thing, and I'd not expect to get anything from me either." He pounded the stick in his hand, no longer caring that it was too little to do much damage. "You touch any of us with that, and this thing between us will be done before you draw back to use it."

Confused, he just stood there. Was Demi telling him to hit her, or was she threatening him? He didn't think she'd be asking for it. To his way of thinking she deserved being hit and more, but before he could work out what he should do, she was in the big limo and gone.

The six men there just stared at him. Nathan looked over at Astrid when they started down the stairs. One of them just picked him up like he didn't weigh close to four hundred pounds. He didn't have any choice but to look at the man when he ordered him to, and Nathan was afraid.

"You come near my family again, any of them, and I will break you in half. Do you understand me?" Nathan nodded, then shook his head. "What is it you don't understand? The family being safe or me killing you?"

"I don't know who your family is to stay away from. I understand the rest of it. I don't care for being threatened, so you know. And if I had my ball bat, I'd show you. But I don't, so you can get off this time." Nathan landed on his ass and knew that he was going to have a difficult time getting upright again. Astrid said he looked like a giant turtle when he did that.

"My family is the McCrays. That would include Demi as well, since she did just marry my brother. Stay away."

They stepped around him as he sat there. And before he could count to ten, they were gone. He and Astrid were the only two around.

"Well, if that don't beat all." Astrid said that they were going to get it. "Yes, but I don't know that we'll be able to take them all on. We'll do it one at a time."

They plotted all the way back to the hotel. Yes, Nathan thought, he needed his trusty ball bat. Or one like it. Demi was going to pay, by God. And so would that man.

~*~

Lucian wanted to kill something. He wouldn't—it was his wedding day—but to have her family come along and put a sour note on their big day really pissed him off. When his mom came into the room with him and smacked him hard on the cheek, he had to work hard to calm his bear.

"You let him go right now and I will have your ass in that shed faster than you can talk your way out of it. You know I will too." He nodded and told her he was sorry. "You'd best be telling that to your new wife. You being in here pouting about not being able to hurt someone that messed up your day is pitiful. What do you think would have happened to you had you hurt that man?"

"He'd be dead." She smacked him again. "Perhaps this would be a good deal faster if you just told me what I should be doing. I know it would be less painful."

"Does she look to you like her day is ruined? Did she

say a word about how she was so angry that she wanted to kill someone?" Lucian looked over where his pretty bride was standing, talking to his brothers, and said that she'd not. "But you think that just because you had someone talk to you badly, it's enough reason for you to stay in this room and not be out there with that lovely wife of yours. I should have beat you more as a child, Lucian. I swear, you are trying my patience today."

"You're right. I have been a sour child." She said she was always right, and he'd be better off when he remembered that. "Yes, I will be. Thanks, Mom. By the way, we're going to have a baby."

He left her there. Lucian could almost see his mom's face as what he'd said to her registered. Lucian found his father and kissed him on the cheek. Demi had told him earlier that he was going to tell his parents, and she would just stand back and watch them scramble to hug him.

"Dad, I have something to tell you." His dad nodded and said that he loved him. "I love you too. Demi and I are going to have a baby soon. We wanted to tell you and Mom first, and—"

The hug took his breath away. Then Dad swung him around the room until he was almost dizzy with it. After putting him down, he looked at the man he most wanted to be like. A father like his dad was, and a man that people respected, but not for what he had in his bank account.

"You just made my whole life with that sentence. I'm telling you son, to be a grandda after being a daddy—well, you just made me the happiest man in the world. Did you tell your mother?" About that time, she grabbed Lucian from behind and hugged him. "I'm guessing you did. Oh my, a grandbaby. What is it? Boy? Girl? You know, I just don't care."

"We don't know the sex as yet. But we did want you to be the first to know. And Mom, you could help Demi a little about this. She's worried that she'll make a terrible mom, just because of the way she grew up without a good role model." Mom said it would be her pleasure, but she thought that she'd do a fine job. "I know that, but she's very worried."

"You leave it to me. Oh, Lucian, this is wonderful news. I'm so happy. Aren't you thrilled, Alden?" Dad kissed Mom on the mouth, and apparently that was all the answer that she needed. "I need to tell someone. Who haven't you told?"

"My brothers." She looked shocked, then she asked if she could tell them. "So long as you have us by your side when you do. Or, why don't you just have Demi there? It will make her feel so much better when she's able to see their reactions right away."

"Good idea." She kissed him again. "I'm just so very happy. A daughter and a grandbaby all in one day. I'm beside myself with happiness."

Mom clapped her hands loudly when she went to get Demi. But before he could watch what was going on, Demi grabbed his hand and held him close to her. Dad joined Mom on the other side. This was going to be epic. He only hoped that his brothers thought so as well.

"I've just had the most wonderful news. Lucian and Demi are going to have a baby." There was silence for a full minute. And in that time, Demi squeezed his hand so tightly he was sure that he'd have broken bones. "Did you hear me? You're all going to be uncles."

The silence was broken by the five of them whooping it up. Each of them gently hugged Demi and thanked her.

She had to ask what they were thanking her for when Pierce spoke.

"For bringing happiness and love into this house again. We all had it, we did. But this, having you a part of the family, I don't know, it feels like we're coming together. I love you, Demi McCray." She smiled and said that was the first time anyone had called her that. "Yes, well, let me be the first to welcome you to the family. Sister dear, we are yours to command. To a point."

They all said the same thing, welcoming her to the family and happy that they were having a child. Lucian was very proud of his brothers. They were gentle with her, and she let them be. In a few days he was sure that she'd take them to task for treating her like a fragile flower. But for now, they were about as happy as they could be.

"We'll be having a dinner at our house tomorrow night. Sort of a moving in kind of thing. I know we tried that before, but you know how life can be. Always cropping up something." Dad cleared his throat. "I would like to say something that's been on my mind for a few days now. I want to say it to Demi." Dad turned to her. "You've given us more than just houses and money in our accounts, love. You've given us happiness that we'd not even known we were missing before. I get up every morning now and don't worry about what bill is not going to be paid. And I go to bed each night thanking the good Lord for bringing you to us when He did. Not for the money, though that has been a big help, but for the love that you've given us. I just don't know what we'd have done had you not come when— I don't think I'm saying this very well."

"Yes, you've said what came from your heart, and that

means so much more to me than if you'd written yourself a speech. And I love you too. I've never had a father before. My mother was...well, you know what she was. You've made it very easy for me to take you to my heart and keep you there. All of you have." She looked around the room, then at Lucian. "And I have the best, most understanding mate and husband in the entire world."

They kissed then. And it occurred to him, like a bolt of lightning hitting him in the heart, that he really did love Demi. Not for her money, like Dad had said, but for her heart. She was the very best thing that could have ever happened to him. And he picked her up, much like his father had him, and swung her around the room.

"I love you so much, Demi McCray. Love you more than anything."

He kissed her again, much to the delight of his family. He loved her. There wasn't anything in the world that could bring him down now. He had a wife, a baby on the way, and a good home to raise all their children in. Lucian couldn't foresee anything getting him down ever again.

Chapter 8

Demi read over the contract. It was straightforward, and the two loopholes that she'd found were not that serious that she'd turn the deal down. The people in town needed this more than she needed to back out of paying off the debt incurred should her end of the deal fail. Such as not having enough people to fill the slots open. She looked at Jamie when he said her name.

"I've been over the property that you suggest. I'm going to have to start over — I think you knew that when you called me about it." She said she had, that the building there was out of date. "It is. And the building isn't fitted for what I need it for anyway. Storage for cars doesn't have a lot of need for conveyer belts."

"Yes, I understand. But you will use some of the people here to help with both the tear down and the construction. From what I've heard there are about a dozen workers here from the last build. And you saw the shape of that one." He said it was good and sound. "The contract mentions expansion. I can see that, Jamie. Custom fitting cars with logo and paint jobs is highly sought after. And the fact that you make it all here is a plus too."

"I agree. And yes, I can see the need for expansion. You've convinced me that I have a very good product that needs to be out there." He laughed when she smiled. "You have a good head on your shoulders. Does that new husband of yours know that?"

"I do." Lucian came in the room with them just in time to hear the question. After kissing her on the mouth, he sat in the chair next to Jamie. "I have an idea that I'd like to pass by you, Jamie. It concerns the dealership you have here in town. Why not fancy up a few of the cars on this lot? You know, make them have every little gadget known to man on them. Show them what the new plant is going to be doing here when you open it. Then take out a full page add that you can have anything you want in your new car. I noticed that the only places that you have that sort of advertising is in the larger cities. With the new businesses coming to town, I think you might be surprised at the people who could come here to see them and perhaps purchase."

"Honestly, I have thought of it, several times, but the management there, prior to your brother, said it wouldn't be a good idea. Putting things in place that people couldn't afford." Jamie pulled out an envelope. "I was looking over the reported sales for that dealership before coming here. Josiah has already hit his sales goal for the entire month. And he still has seventeen days to go. He's only been there for a week and a half, and I can already tell a difference is being made."

"Yes, I've noticed that as well. The other day I saw that the cars were being washed up. I hadn't realized how dirty they were before. But they shine, don't they? And the special that he's running right now is smart." Demi leaned back while Lucian went on about his brother. "To have someone test drive a car and get to have their own car washed and detailed is wonderful. I think he sold two cars the first day."

"Yes, he called me and asked if I had a problem with it. I thought it was brilliant and told him so. Then he hit me up for a power washer. Really, Josiah wanted to rent one for a few days, to spray off the building and the cars. But then he told me the prices of them compared to renting one every couple of weeks to wash cars. It seems to me that he was being held back there before. Hiring him as manager was a good idea, Demi. Thank you."

"All I wanted to do was provide transportation for my family. Josiah is a good salesman too. Not just the cars but having the people who work with him know that they are as well." Jamie thanked her again as she finished up with the contract. "Jamie, I'm looking for another business to come in. Know anyone that would like to place a distribution plant here? The one that is here now is going to close up at the end of the fiscal period. That's in two months, and two hundred plus people will be out of work."

"Not distribution, no. But I have heard of a place that is wishing to expand soon. I think it's the capital that is holding them back." She wrote down the name of the company. "I think I read just a few days ago that their stock is at an all-time low. I bought up a few shares of it myself."

"You knew that I'd help." He said that he had hoped she would. "I'll do some research on it. And in the future, if you need anything, you can ask Lucian here. He's my partner in all this."

109

Jamie said that he had a meeting in his home state that evening and left. Demi asked Lucian if he was willing to be her partner in her businesses. He grinned like a kid at his own birthday party.

"I haven't any idea what he was talking about most of the time, just so you know. The stock prices I understand. I see them on the afternoon news. But why did he buy shares when they're low? And what does being low have to do with a business trouble? I know what capitol is, but why would he mention that to you?" Lucian laughed. "I would be the worse partner anyone ever took on, don't you think? I don't know enough to help you at all, love."

"You know a great deal. You saw that the cars were washed, and the building was also clean. You kept up on the event that your brother was having. That shows that you're interested. And you had a suggestion for Jamie. That helps him and us when we work together." Lucian said it was his brother. "Regardless, you knew about it. And as a partner, you'd notice the things going on with our businesses because it's our money they're using."

"Okay, that makes sense. And the rest of this, you'll hopefully explain more as we go along, right?" She nodded at him. "Okay, tell me what he meant."

"Capitol. You said you knew that it was what the company in question has ahead of what they owe. But they need more to expand in order to either hit goals or to bring in more product to sell. In this case, a bank will more than likely turn them down flat. One, because their stock is going down. Two, because they're a fairly new business that is still getting their feet wet in the industry." Demi pulled the company up on her computer. Their stock was down. "Jamie knew that if he told me about the company and I thought it was a good investment, the low stocks that he bought would be worth a great deal more if we, our company, stepped in and helped them out. Buy low, sell high. That's what we'd do as well. But since we're going to help them, buying their stock first would hurt us in the long run. People, the government, would see it as insider work. And I don't work that way. We won't work that way."

Lucian asked a lot of good questions about stocks and how they worked. She watched the stock go down another point and looked at that. The company's holders, the people on the board, were dumping it. She said that they could buy it and own the company. That would be different than just buying a few shares to make some money.

"So, if you own it—" She told him that they would own it. "Okay, if we own it, then the stocks are all right to purchase. I don't understand."

"If we're buying the stock to take over the business, then that's fine. Yes, we're making a profit, but in a way that takes some money and hard work. We have an investment in it now, not just a purchase for gain. Understand?" He said that he did, so she purchased all seven hundred shares of the stock. "We now own the company. No one will be able to tell us yes or no to things we might wish to change, or that we have to close down the place. It'll be our decision to make, and no one can stop us."

"Do you think you'll have to close it down?" She said she'd not know until she got there. "So, without knowing anything about this company, you bought it up. Isn't that a little risky?"

"Yes. And while I rarely do this, I have a gut feeling that

111

this is going to be the way to go with this company. And because we own the most shares, we'll be able to put the expansion anywhere we want. Like here in this town."

They worked together until supper time. The dinner at his parents' house was at six, and they decided to walk over rather than drive. The evening was turning into a nice one, and the trees were just beginning to turn. A touch of cooler weather was nice.

"I've spoken to my brothers about your mom's house. They're going to decide if they want it or not. I don't think I'd hold out much hope on that however." Demi told him that she didn't care. It would make a nice rental. "Yes, that's what Gannon said. Did you know that he's lost his job at the mall? And that the people that own it — the mall, I mean — they're going to be closing it down soon too."

"I heard. There isn't much use for a mall per se anymore. People do more shopping online rather than go out into the world. It would make a nice place to put a school. High school, I mean." She had gone to school here, a long time ago, and had thought the place was outdated even then. "Perhaps when we get enough businesses coming in, we'll hit them up for donations to have their name put on it. And there is need for a sports field, as well as a locker room for them."

"You've given this town a great deal of thought, haven't you?" Demi told Lucian that she'd given a lot of things a great deal of thought around here. "Your grandma would have been very proud of you, Demi. You know that, don't you?"

"Oh yes, I know. When I came to visit her, I'd have to just go to her home and then back to mine so that I'd not be found by my brother or sister. I didn't want my grandma to see me hurt again, so I'd avoid seeing them. I more than likely could have taken them on, but to see me battered again, I don't think she would have taken that well." He asked her about seeing her mom. "No, I never went to see her. She was instrumental in me getting hurt all the time. She'd either egg them on or just stand back while they did it. The letter that she gave me at the end of her life, it was well meant, I'm sure, but it wouldn't have changed my mind about her or anything that she'd done to me."

"No, I would guess not. I don't know how I'd feel, honestly. She and the rest of your family, they didn't deserve you. Or anything you might have been able to do for them." Demi nodded, not really wanting to talk about it anymore. "Demi, what did your brother mean by you owing them? For the life of me, I can't figure that out."

"Neither have I. I believe they've found out about me paying for the upkeep on the house. Alan told me the other day they were making inquiries around town. Not that I care what information they have. That is a done deal." Lucian asked her what she was going to do about them. "I really don't have any idea. My first thought was to just run them out of town. But that won't work. They have no money, nor do they have the health to find them a job. Nathan is just days from having a massive stroke. Astrid is close as well, but not nearly so much as Nathan. And I believe that they're both diabetic, from being so overweight and not watching anything that they put in their mouths."

"I've seen that. When we got the bill from the hotel where they're staying, I did wonder for a few minutes if they had had a band come by and stay with them. Turns out it was just the two of them." They laughed just as they were on the decking around his parents' house. "Demi, I love you very

113

much. And whatever you want to do about this, I'm here for you."

"Thank you, Lucian. You have no idea how comforting that is to hear all the time." He kissed her. "You keep that up and we'll never make it to dinner."

"I'd like to say we should just forget it, but my mom would have my head. We can't even use the excuse that we're making a baby for her." They were laughing when they went inside. "To be honest with you, I'm not sure if we're supposed to knock anymore. This isn't my old house."

"You knock, and I'll knock you in the head." Alden hugged them both as he continued. "Your mom is cooking up a storm in that new kitchen of hers. I swear, she'd just been holding back until she got one that suited her. There are five pies, son. And a cake. We are also having hot bread out of that machine you sent us over. My goodness, a man could be very happy with all the gadgets that we have now."

"No dying off." He hugged her again. They all followed the smells to the kitchen. Everyone else was already there. "Goodness, you guys sure do fill up a room. What can I do to help?"

She didn't get to help—they were still in the pampering mood and she allowed it. But tomorrow she was going to put her foot down—or her fist. Whatever worked the quickest. Demi did love this family.

~*~

Lucian was trying his best to make heads or tails out of the blueprints he'd picked up this morning. The building was where it was supposed to be, but the rest of it was just garbage for him. Turning it once again, he looked over at Ian when he laughed.

114

"I'm sure that if you turn it once more, you'll be more confused." Lucian handed it to him. "All right, but you owe me lunch for this. You're not holding it wrong, but you aren't looking at the first page."

They put the sheaths of paper on a nearby table. When Ian had it on the front page, Lucian could see the outside of the building the way it was suppose to have been—the proposed flowers and trees that seemed to have not made it to the grounds, and the parking lot that was much larger than the one that had been built. He wasn't sure how the smaller parking lot was going to affect the plant, but they could enlarge it with the land that surrounded it.

"I thought that it was all the same and you just had to figure out which one to look at." Ian told him that was almost right. That the blueprints were done in layers. "So they do the first page and move onto the second?"

"No, more like last to first. See?" Lucian did see then. It wasn't that he was reading it wrong, he was just reading it too deeply. All he wanted to find out was how many bathrooms the place had per square foot. "That's easier. See this chart here? It tells you how many bathrooms there are, as well if they're male or female or both. There is also a place in the breakrooms for hands to be washed up. It says that there are fridges in here too, but I've never seen one."

The distribution center that had been about to close had abruptly closed their doors yesterday evening. The second shift had come in to work and been turned away. They were also told that the stuff they had inside their lockers would be boxed up in several days. That wasn't going to happen either, as the lockers, along with several of the large dining tables, had already been taken away by some unknown hand.

"We bought the building as of this morning so that we could change the locks on the door." Ian said he didn't lose anything, but a few of his friends had. "I'm sorry about that. I really am. Ian, I have to tell you something. I'm scared out of my mind about this stuff. We paid seven million dollars for this place. Seven million. And Demi bought it thinking she'd gotten a deal. All this money going out and neither of us working is making me sleepless at night."

"You should talk to Demi. I know that there is money coming in too, by the way. Me working for you guys, it's given me a firsthand look at all the income you guys have. I don't know where it goes after I put it on the ledger for her, but there is money." Lucian told Ian that's what Demi had said. "Lucian, she's been doing this longer than we have—being rich, I mean. You should be assured that she's not going to let you guys go broke. If anything, she's making you more money than you could spend in several lifetimes. Trust her."

It was hard for him to have money like he did and not worry about it. He supposed that Demi worried too. She was at the computer a great deal, looking at contracts and trying to get people to back her ideas. Demi never seemed to have anyone turn her down on ideas either. Her biggest supporter was some man by the name of Prince A. Jovanni. She had an interview with him tomorrow evening. He was coming to their home.

"This Prince guy, he's been here before. I guess he's backed her on several deals that have made them both a ton of money. Did you know that she has investments in things overseas as well?" Ian said that he had an idea that she did. "Yes, well, coffee. And chocolate. I didn't know you could invest in chocolate. But there is a big market for it."

"Because there are a lot of males fucking up with their wives, I guess." Ian laughed with him as he pointed out a couple of things on the plans. "You might want to tell Demi that the second floor of this place isn't on these blueprints. And it looks as if it was added much later."

They were going up the stairs when the stairs started to sway. It took both of them by surprise enough that they went back down them without going up. If this was the workmanship on this place, he was concerned that the place would be a work hazard rather than a good place to open up.

"I'd just tear it down and start over. Or it could have swayed because you and I aren't exactly lightweights either." They weren't. Both of them, because of their other selves, weighed about a hundred pounds more than a human would at their height.

He made notes on the tablet that he'd been carrying around. It had a nice program on it so that he could simply type or use a special pen to write himself notes. And he had files, a great many of them, that he could pull up and look over. Demi had been sending him things to look over since he'd gotten it. Once she read something over, she'd send it to him to have a look too. And since he told her that he didn't know what he was looking at, she'd begun marking it in places that he needed to be aware of. It certainly made it easier on him, and she'd not made fun of him once for it.

"Lucian, I was thinking that you and I could go running tonight. The property behind your house is perfect for it."

"I'd love that. And if you don't mind, Demi wants to get to know each of our bears. She said that she doesn't want to come up on one of us and not know the difference." Ian agreed, saying that they should all get her scent too. "I'll ask her."

As a newly married spouse, he'd been asking instead of telling. Demi hadn't said anything to him when he'd first started telling her what he wanted her to do. Like the first day after they were living together. He'd told her that he made the bed when he was the last one in, sort of hinting that she might want to take up the practice herself. But then he realized, quite stupidly, that neither of them had to make the bed because that was what the staff was for. He had apologized all that day to anyone that he saw in the household, feeling awful for forgetting about them. They had just looked at him like his cheese had slipped right off his cracker.

He was learning to share his things too. Demi would wear his shirts to bed at times. He found that it didn't bother him as much as he thought it would. And when she would come into where he was and sit on his lap with just his shirt on, Lucian would get hard in an instant.

He had his notes all in order by the time he got home. They were going to open an office for them to use in town soon. It would make it so they weren't always going back and forth to the house when they needed to get something done. It was a forty-minute drive to town from their home.

When he pulled into the drive, he was surprised to find a taxi just dropping someone off. Turned out it was Astrid.

"Just the person I wanted to see." Instead of going inside and inviting her in, he sat down on one of the rockers that was there. "You're not going to invite me in? Offer me a cup of tea or a glass of water? That's very antisocial of you. What would my sister say if she knew you were treating me this way?"

"She'd probably pat me on the back and ask you what the fuck you want." Which he knew she would. But it put Astrid off, and he could see her struggling with her temper. "So, what the fuck do you want? Money? Not happening. Food? Nope. I'd watch you starve. Anything else? No, you're not getting that either."

"What the hell did I do to you? Or are you always in a mood like this one? You and Demi must make a pair, the two of you nipping and biting at people." She stomped over to the other rocker and tried to sit in it. Her ass was much too wide for her to fit, he saw. Instead of laughing like he wanted to do, he just watched her. She was much too close for his comfort.

"What is it, Astrid? I'm a very busy man, and I have no trouble calling the cops to have them escort you off our land." Astrid told him he was a fucking bastard. "Perhaps it's just you bringing out the worst in me. Again, what is it you want?"

"Money. A great deal of it too. My sister has enough to toss around like it's nothing to her. Well, we want a cut of it. It's the least that she could do after having us thrown from our family home." Lucian pointed out that she'd paid for it, the taxes and repairs, and it had been her family home too. "No, you have that all wrong. She was never a part of our family. Not then anyway."

"So, she's only a part of your family when it's convenient for you and Nathan. I'm afraid that I don't see it that way. Both of you should have been tossed out the moment that *my wife* paid the back taxes and had your mother getting the best of care. Despite what she did to her for all those years. Demi did more for the three of you than I think you deserved." She snorted at him. "You have a different opinion? Please, tell me, were you there when she was beaten with a whip? How about the time that you poured scalding water over her feet when she said that they were cold? Or how about — ?"

"Yes, I was there. Christ, did she tell you every fucking thing? Not that it matters. She should have given us money too when she was giving Mommy all those drugs and shit to help her. It was a total waste of money anyway. She did die, didn't she? That money could have gone for better things. Like Nathan and I a better home. My hair and nails done on a regular basis instead of when I could sell something off. Christ, they say she's the richest woman in the world. What would she miss if you give us a couple million of your half?"

"I own just as much as she does. Everything that she's made or owns is now mine." Astrid stumbled back from him when he stood up. "Now, you'll see that I'm being very polite right now in asking you to get the fuck out of here. The next time I say it, I'm going to chase you all the way down the driveway."

Astrid did just what he'd hoped that she would. And when he stepped off the porch he watched her face as he asked her once more.

"I'm not leaving here without money, you fucking prick. You had nothing before she felt sorry for you and took you under her wing. What do you think she's going to do when she's sick of the trash you call a family?" He said nothing but did pull off his belt. "What do you think you're going to do, fuck me?"

"Hell no."

He let his bear take him. And when she screamed, he laughed to himself. This might be just what his bear needed to feel good about helping their mate. And he did just what he'd threatened to do, too. He chased her all the way down the long drive, even waiting for her to waddle her way up off the ground when she fell. He was still laughing as he made his

120

way back to the house. He'd do that again if Nathan showed up. However, he'd take a bit of help, like a crane, to get up once he fell.

Lucian couldn't wait to tell Demi. He hoped that she'd not be mad at him for doing it. Now that he thought on it, it was her sister after all.

When he got to the house, she was sitting on the chair he'd been in, laughing so hard that all he got from her was that she'd been in the house. And she'd apparently been watching. He asked her if she was angry with him.

"Christ no, I'm not mad. I wish I could have seen the whole thing. But I have to tell you, I was laughing so hard I might have had to have you help me up a couple of times. Oh, Lucian. You have made my day with this." They went into the house. "Now we wait for them both to come here. And they will. They are too stupid to think that this is the end of it."

Lucian didn't care. It was fun and funny to deal with her sister, and the fact that Demi wasn't mad made him feel better. The next time, Demi told him, she was going to follow them. Just to record it for their next family get together.

Life with this woman would never be the expected. He was happier every moment that she'd come into his life.

Chapter 9

Nathan couldn't believe his sister. Not that he thought she was lying, but the fact that his McCray person had been a bear all along. That should be worth some money to them. He'd tell them to give it over or they'd tell the entire town. They might anyway, he'd told Astrid.

"I'm telling you right now, Nathan, that man tried to murder me. I could see him licking his chops every time that I...that I had to see if he was behind me." He knew that she'd fallen a great deal. Her clothing was dirty, and her knees were all scratched up. Nathan wasn't sure he'd look any different, but he would have wet himself for sure. "The next time I go see them about money, I'm taking a fucking gun with me."

"We don't have one." That had earned him a smack on the back. Astrid had been getting more and more violent towards him daily. He supposed it was the stress of everything going on, but that didn't mean he had to like it. "Oh, before I forget to tell you again, the manager came by just a little while ago. Apparently, Demi has been paying for our room, and he said she called and said she was done with it. Even the little fridge that we have, we have to pay for that too if we eat from it."

In his stress about the money again, Nathan had not only cleared it out, but had begged for it to be filled up again so that Astrid didn't know. But in his haste to make the thing look full, he'd gotten scared again and had nearly emptied it. Now his belly was sick.

"She's been paying it all along and she can just go on paying for it. I'll have to add that to my list for when I see her again. Damn it, Nathan, that man scared me half to death with his changing thing." It was a good idea, but he didn't think it was going to work. Demi, he noticed, was pretty stubborn nowadays. "We'll both go out there tomorrow. I don't know how we'll pay for the taxi again, but we'll figure something out. Maybe we can write a check to this place and have them give us the cash for it."

"I tried that already, remember? They said that the bank is across the street and they're not affiliated." He'd had to ask Astrid what that meant. "I'm thinking that someone is telling people not to help us, Astrid. Just this morning after you left, I went down to the little shop. They told me that we weren't allowed in their store anymore. That without cash up front, they weren't to do business with us. You thinking that was Demi?"

"Yes. Who else could it be but her? She's certainly gotten uppity, don't you think? Like she can not only tell us off but tell us what we're to do. Did I tell you her husband threatened to call the police on me?" He said that she had told him, four times now. "Well, I'll tell you again and again if I feel like it. I'm her fucking sister. I can't be arrested for being on her land, as he called it."

124

Since Nathan wasn't sure that was right either, he kept his mouth shut. There were times, like now, that it was smarter to just let Astrid rant a bit. Then when she'd had enough, you could talk to her. But not until then.

Astrid bitched and moaned for another hour. Nathan was starving now that his belly had time to rest. He wanted a couple of fat burgers and fries. Even a milk shake wouldn't be too bad. The television had some kind of cooking channel on, and he wanted to try everything that had been made. Even the things that didn't look like they would taste good.

By nine-thirty they'd tried all three pizza places to get a pie delivered to them. Nobody was working with them on this. And when Astrid said she'd flash them her tits—her words, not his—the man had told her that he'd rather have a hot pie on his dick than to have to see that image burnt into his mind.

There wasn't any reason that he could see that anyone would insult Astrid like that. He'd not want to see them either, but he was her brother, and that thought sort of made him ill. So they were both sitting on the beds wondering what they were going to do now.

They had no money—not a single dime between them. The fridge was empty, thanks to him, and Astrid had knocked him around for five minutes because of it. She might have gone on longer, but she had some chest pains that that scared them both. But after she settled down, Astrid told him that she felt a lot better.

"What are we going to do now?" Astrid told him she was thinking. "Okay, I'll sit here and think too. It might make my belly stop protesting."

It didn't. Nathan thought it was worse. He'd never been

a real thinker, and all he could think about was food. It was no different now. So, getting up, he made his way to the little table next to the window. He might have sat down, but the first night there he'd busted the other chair all to pieces and needed three men help him up. Something was going to have to happen about his weight, he told himself.

He saw Demi and that man again, headed to the store across from the hotel. He almost hid back out of the way but remembered that she knew they were here. Going to the door just as Astrid went to the bathroom, he didn't even tell her that he was going out. Closing the door softly behind him, he made his way to street level before he had to take a breather. He wasn't able to ride the elevator because of the weight limit and his fear of people wanting to get on with him. It was a terror that he would crash to the bottom and be nothing more than a splat of fat on the floor. It could hold up to a couple of thousand pounds, sure, but he knew that it would make all kinds of moaning sounds and creaks before it even started. So, he took the stairs every time after that.

Going out of the building, he put his hand over his heart, trying to calm it down before talking to his sister. They were shopping. He didn't have any idea what it was they were looking at; they seemed to have circled the store twice before he got to them. Nathan was having a hard time breathing now and sat down on one of the recliners that was in the shop. Finally, he had to put his head between his legs — well, his head down, anyway — before he passed out. He saw the shoes when he opened his eyes.

"I just need a minute. I've had a hard day." The man told him to look at him. "Just a minute. I need to catch my breath."

Only he couldn't. Not only couldn't he catch his breath,

but his chest was feeling like someone was squeezing the shit out of him. When he finally looked up at the man, he had to work hard at making out which one he was.

"You're having a heart attack. Just stay with me, Nathan." He wanted to nod, but he was feeling sick again. "Demi is calling for an ambulance for you. Just don't pass out on me. Or fall. I don't think they'll be able to lift you on their own. My brothers are on their way."

"They going to kill me?" He thought it was a reasonable question, but the man didn't answer. "I'm hurting powerfully bad. You're Demi's husband."

"Yes, Lucian McCray. You're Nathan Morgan." He said he was. "All right, Nathan, I have to ask you a few questions. The hospital wants to know. When did you last eat?"

"A couple of hours ago. Candy and stuff from the fridge in the hotel room. We don't have any real food in there. Are you sure someone is coming to help? I'm not sure how much longer I can stay up." Lucian told him to hang on. "I'm trying. Talk to me please. Tell me about Demi."

"She's the most wonderful human being I've ever met. I love her with all my heart, and then some. And she is going to have my child." Nathan felt his own heart hurt. Not from the attack on it, but that someone could love his sister that much. "Nathan, open your eyes."

He'd not realized that he'd closed them. But he was getting weaker all the time. And when he tried to lift his arm up, it wouldn't budge. He asked the man standing in front of him about it, completely forgetting his name again.

"Lucian. And you just hang on, buddy. I can hear the ambulance now. Can you?" He tried to speak, but his words sounded all garbled to him. "Nathan, stay with me. Don't you die on me, you hear me?"

"I don't want to die. I'm fat. I was going to have one of those things put in my belly so that I'd get skinny again. I used to be." Lucian asked him if he really wanted to get thinner. "I do. I really do. I'm tired of.... Lucian, I don't think I'm going to make it."

Nathan felt himself slipping when he was suddenly pulled up. He asked where he was when the man in white told him that he was taking him to the hospital. Nathan was sure that he'd died, and this was an angel.

"No. I'm just an EMT, sir. And we have all your information from your sister, Demi. Now there is a good woman. Did you know that she's helping us with a fundraiser to get another ambulance? Without her help with this one, we'd not be able to save you, I'm afraid. Now you stand a better chance." He hoped what he was saying was right, because Nathan did not want to die. "I just need you to be still for me. Lucian and his brothers are going ahead of us to help us carry you in. Had they not been there to help, I'm not sure what we would have done."

"He told me that he loved Demi." The man said that Lucian was a very lucky man to have found his other half. "Yes, I think he is. Does she love him?"

"Oh yes. They're going to be having a baby. Hey, that will make you an uncle. What do you think of that?" He was starting to feel better — not great, but better — and told the man he thought he was going to be all right. "No, you're having a heart attack, Mr. Morgan. You're only feeling better because we've been giving you something to help you along. Once you get to the hospital, they'll do everything they can to save your life. You just listen to them and do what they tell you, and you'll get to hold your new niece or nephew."

Once the ambulance stopped or something like that happened, Nathan felt himself being lifted up. There were the four men that he'd seen on the courthouse steps, and they were lifting him into the hospital. After that they stood by but didn't help the rest of the people running around the little cubical with him. It was sickening, really, to see so many blurs, so he let himself fall under the medication.

"Mr. Morgan?" He tried to open his eyes, but his body didn't feel like it was ever going to work right again. And he couldn't make his mouth work to say anything. "All right, Mr. Morgan, I'll have your sister sign off on your paperwork. We're going to put you under now, and then we're going to take you to the operating room. We need to do some work on your heart to make it work again."

"Not working?" It was the best that he could do, and the man seemed to understand. He told him that nothing in his heart was working right because he was so overweight. "Fat."

"Yes, well, I was trying to be polite. You're going to start to feel lightheaded. You just let the meds do what they're for, and soon you're going to be in recovery if things go all right." Nathan tried to ask him if he thought they would, but the drugs hit his system like a large hunk of apple pie with mounds of whipped cream and ice cream. Then he felt nothing else. Nathan was sure that he'd died.

~*~

Lucian sat with Demi while they waited on the police to bring in Astrid. They didn't think that Nathan was going to make it. He was not only well over his weight guidelines, but he was in poor health too. He thought about the list of things that they'd found out about Nathan in the quick exam in the emergency room.

"I'm afraid that he's left his diabetes unchecked for so long that he will need to be put on a strict diet or it will kill him. He has sores on his legs and buttocks that have been infected for some time." The doctor went on to describe the hygiene of the man, and how his weight was keeping him from bathing properly. "Having this heart attack isn't anything that unexpected. Mr. Morgan was lucky that he'd not had one well before now. We're going to have to work on his heart, first and foremost. After that, we'll talk about getting him on a proper diet and exercise program."

Lucian stood up when they heard the wailing of Astrid. She was screaming about what Demi had done to her poor brother, and how she was going to sue her for everything. As soon as she got within touching distance, she drew back her fist to no doubt hit Demi. But his wife spoke first.

"You hit me right now, Astrid, and even in the hospital they'll never be fast enough to save you. I will kill you where you stand. Now sit down and shut the fuck up before I have to do it for you. And so you are aware, I am not in the mood to fuck around with you right this minute."

Astrid hesitated, just for a moment, then sat down. Demi did as well, but he remained standing.

"What did you do to him? I'm sure whatever is going on, it's all your fault." Demi calmly told her what was going on and why Nathan might not make it. "You killed him, just like you did our mother. I hate you, Demi. You're nothing but a fucking bitch, and a liar."

Lucian started to slap Astrid himself when his father jerked the woman up from the seat she was perched on and slapped her hard enough to turn her head. When she looked at his dad, Astrid growled at him. Dad, being a bear, simply growled, much louder and longer, back at her.

"Now you will listen up, or so help me young lady, I will do things to you that even your worst nightmare won't have covered. I'm not usually a violent man, but you bring that out in people." Dad stretched his neck and then glared at Astrid. "Had my son and Demi not been there with him, Nathan would have surely died. And when we got here with him, that nice doctor was told to get the best to come in here and take care that your brother gets the best care. They didn't do a thing other than go shopping, where he came to them. You had better get all your facts in a row before you go accusing this family of wrong doings, or so help me, I'll take you to that woodshed out back and you'll never come out. Now, you sit there and shut that mouth of yours until someone asks you a question. We've had a stressing time, and for now, I'm willing to think that's what has your knickers in a twist."

When Astrid sat down, Demi stood up and hugged his dad. They were very close, and Lucian felt wonderful about their relationship. But when she asked him what the hell knickers were, the rest of them burst out laughing. It eased the tension a great deal.

The surgery was going to take several hours. That was what concerned the doctor so much — the stress of the surgery on Nathan's already worn out body. But as the minutes ticked by, so did their hope. No one, not one member of his family, wanted to see the man die, but he'd better straighten his act up or there would be hell to pay.

"Let's take a walk." Demi nearly leapt from the chair she was in when he made the suggestion. They were at the elevator when his mom joined them, asking if it was all right that she did. "Of course. I just thought a breath of fresh air might be good."

They were outside in the little park when Mom started talking. It was as if she had piled up everything she wanted to say in one breath. The dialogue started out about the baby and ended up with Nathan and Astrid.

"I'm sorry. I've had that on my mind for some time." Demi said she could tell and hugged her. "The things that woman said to you. I just cannot believe that you are from the same gene pool. I've heard that said before, several times on the television but I never understood it until this very moment. My goodness, she is a horrid person, isn't she? But I have to say, had your father not gotten to her before me, she would have been in some serious hurt."

"She and Nathan have always been that way. I haven't any idea why. I mean, other than my mom would egg them on a great deal. She would even watch over them as they beat the shit out of me. But why me? I haven't any idea." Demi leaned back, closing her eyes to the sun shining on her face. "I never knew my father all that well. He passed away when I was about five. My grandmother had the most amazing stories about him as a child. But as he grew older, married to Abrielle, he became this person she didn't know. Not like them, but somewhat a shell of his former self. Grandma told me once that I was nothing like him. He was a man who waited for things to come to him. He wasn't lazy, but he wasn't that ambitious either. Grandma blamed that on being battened down by marriage to his wife."

"Have you always called her by her first name? Your mother, I mean." Lucian had noticed that the other two called their mother Mommy, like they were still children and hadn't grown up. Before Demi could answer him, a nurse came out to tell them that the doctor wished to see them. They were in the elevator when Demi answered him.

"Yes, always. I mean, I might have called her mom at first, but she told me that she didn't want to be my mother and hated me, so I shouldn't be allowed to call her something that she wasn't. So, I've been calling her by her first name since I was...I guess I was about seven when I was told to call her Abrielle." Lucian took her hand when she reached for his. "Do you think he didn't make it? Astrid is going to have a fit if he didn't."

"You let me handle Astrid. You just deal with the doctor, all right?" She nodded at him and told him that she loved him. "And I love you as well. Forever."

Everyone was standing near an open door when they got off the elevator. Astrid was there too, shouting out orders to anyone that would listen to her. No one was, apparently, so Lucian ignored her as well. She was telling people that he'd better have the best or she'd have their jobs. Like that was going to happen.

"The surgery went as well as can be expected. His heart was in worse shape than we first thought it would be. He now has a pacemaker, as well as some other equipment to make his heart beat stronger — at least until we can get the weight off of him. Some of his bowel was badly damaged, and we had to remove a large portion of it before we could operate on his heart. It would have infected everything that we've done had we not." Demi said that she understood. Astrid was wailing again, talking about how they'd ruined her brother, when one of his own brothers took her away. She was silent after that, much to the happiness of the rest of them. "He will need to be in the hospital for a while. Rehabilitation is going to be long and hard for him. Nathan will need to learn to eat better. Someone here will teach him to take his medications for his diabetes and other issues he'll have. Not to say that he's out of the woods. The next forty-eight hours will be difficult for all of you."

The doctor suggested that they go home, and Demi said that she'd like that. After making sure that the doctor had her phone number and that the front desk did as well, they went to find Astrid. She was sitting next to Ian, who was holding her hand very tightly. Lucian was sure that Astrid was in pain, but she only sat there.

"We're going home." Her sister looked at Demi when she spoke. "You can stay or not, I don't really care. But it's been a really long day, and I just—"

"You're not going to just leave him here, are you?" Demi asked her what she thought she could do by staying. "He's your fucking brother. You have to stay with him. You weren't there when Mommy died. The least you can do is be by my side when I lose the only family I have left."

"In the event that it escaped that addled mind of yours, I'm your sister. And why would you assume that he's going to die? The doctor explained— Oh wait, you missed it because you're a fucking cunt. And I don't use that word often, Astrid, but you bring out the worst in me too. I'll pay for the hotel for two more nights for you. After that, you'll be on your own."

Astrid looked around at his family. "Did you hear that? See what sort of sister she is? My brother is lying in the other room, more than likely dying because of her, and she won't even foot the bill for me so that I can stay close to him." Astrid looked at Lucian. "It's not too late for you to run. I would if I were you, before she murders you as well."

"I love her. And with the baby coming along, I couldn't be more—"

"Baby? You're having a baby? Mother fuck, you have to be the stupidest person alive, Demi. A baby? Christ, the next thing you'll be telling me is that you're going to bury my brother next to a city dump. And think that's where he belongs." Astrid started laughing. It was maniacal and scary. Demi smiled at him and said she was ready to go. "Just go. Abandon us in our hour of need. Isn't that what you always do?"

Demi asked, politely, for him to wait one moment. He was sure she was going to tell her sister off—it was no less than Astrid deserved. But when Demi drew back, punching the heavy woman, who fell back and broke three chairs while she was at it, Demi turned to them and said if they were ready, so was she.

No one said a word as they rode down in the elevator. There wasn't a word spoken as they walked to the parking garage and found their cars. But as soon as Demi and he were in their car, she broke down. It was the hardest thing he'd ever done not to be able to fix how she was feeling right now.

She cried for most of the ride home. He asked her, several times, if he could do anything, and she finally told him to give her time. Lucian knew that everyone had their breaking point, and apparently, Demi had hit hers today.

"It's funny, isn't it?" He glanced at her when she spoke as he drove. "I did nothing but try my best to make things better for all of them, at a great cost to myself. Not money. There was quite a bit, but that wasn't it. It hurt me in ways that I couldn't talk to anyone about. They never cared for me. None of them. Abrielle did at the end, but it was too little too late, I think. And now this. Now I'm being accused once again of holding back on what I could provide for them. Not once, not in all my life, did any of them say to me, 'Thanks.' Or even, 'What can I do to repay you?' The lottery ticket, I suppose, would be something, but again, it was too little too late."

"She gave the money to you because she knew that Nathan and Astrid would have pissed it all away. I'm not saying that it was right of Abrielle to treat you that way, but she did find it in her heart to help someone else at the end." Demi agreed with him, telling him that the money would go a long way in helping people. "And this might not be such a big deal, but it seems that your grandma and mother might have made up at the end."

"No, they didn't. Grandma went to visit her a few times, but it was never cordial. Mostly they fought over my mother's treatment of me. But at some point, they did talk, Grandma told me. It was then that Abrielle told her that she'd won the lottery and her plans for it. That was when Grandma told her about me. Before, Abrielle would ask and all Grandma would tell her was that I was doing well. I guess it was quite a shock to Abrielle that I'd done so well." He asked if she'd asked about getting money from her. "No. Grandma thought it was then that Abrielle figured out how she was getting such good care. And the house was up to date on taxes and such. Lucian, it felt wonderful hitting Astrid, but also sad. I don't want to be like them."

"Never. You'll never be like them. You want to know why I know that? Because you have a giving and wonderful heart. But as I said, everyone has a breaking point, and you hit yours. I'm just surprised that you hadn't hit it long before now." They both laughed and pulled up in front of the house. "I was just thinking. Why don't we not go home, finish our shopping, have a nice dinner in town, and stay nearer the hospital? It'll do us both some good to be able to do something different."

"All right. I love that." Lucian started the car and stopped backing around when she said his name. "I want you to change me. I don't know if you can do it while I'm having a baby, but soon, all right?"

"Yes, all right. I'll talk to my parents and see about how it could harm the baby, and we'll work it out."

He moved down the long drive as Demi called the house to tell them what they were doing. When she laid back on the seat, closing her eyes, Lucian knew that they were going to have to deal with Astrid sooner rather than later. She was, as his dad would say, off her noodle.

Chapter 10

Nathan felt like opening his eyes was the most exhausting thing he'd ever done. He wasn't sure where he was or what had happened, but when he finally got one of them opened, he still had no idea where he was.

"Hello, Nathan." He tried to think who the woman was standing next to him. "It's Demi. You've been out for a few days. Are you going to stay awake this time?"

"What?" That was all he could manage to get out. His head felt like it had been pulled off and set aside for now, and he couldn't move his arms or legs. He opened his eyes when Demi said his name again. "What hap—?"

"You had a heart attack twelve days ago. Do you remember that?" He couldn't shake his head, but she seemed to understand. "You came to see me in the store, and Lucian, my husband, helped you until help got there. You're very lucky to be alive."

He tried to move his arms, and she told him that he had been fighting people and had to be restrained. Demi told him that if he was awake for more than ten minutes and promised to be good, she'd have them released. Nathan was just too tired to fight and let himself drift away again.

The next time he opened his eyes, Nathan felt a little better. At least he was able to open his eyes easily, he thought. Looking around the room, he saw Demi asleep on a recliner, as well as a man that he vaguely remembered. He was awake and watching him.

"Lucian. Demi's husband." He remembered some of the time in the store now, but not a great deal. "Demi is resting. She's been here since you were taken off life support a few days ago. She needs to be here, and if you make her cry again, all the meds in the world will not take away the hurt I put you in."

"Sorry." Lucian nodded and picked up the chair he had been in and brought it close to the bed. "I don't hurt too much. Am I all right?"

"No. Not by a long shot. You have been into surgery twice since they brought you in. Once to repair your heart as best they could. The second time to take care of some damage that happened because you're a type two diabetic, and you've not taken care of yourself." He knew that. His last doctor's appointment had revealed that to him. "I'm to understand that you knew you were a diabetic."

"Yes. Didn't care so much. I should have, but I didn't." Lucian didn't say anything, but Nathan had a feeling that he had a lot to tell him. He was just trying to figure out how to say it. "Demi all right?"

"Yes. She's worn out, as you can imagine. As I said before, she's been here since you were put into this room. By the way, she's paying for all this, so you'd better be grateful to her and not piss me off."

"Grateful? What do you mean, be grateful to her?" Lucian said that he had already been an ungrateful shit and had been all her life. "I'm not sure I remember anything recent. I know that I have been mean to her before. But she made it easy." He thought about that. "I'm sorry. Not right. I made it easy for me."

"Are you having a change of heart about Demi?" Was he? Probably not. Just the drugs, he told himself. "Not that it matters one way or the other. You are going to see some changes when you get out of here. But not for a while yet. You've lost your right leg. I'm not being cruel about how I'm telling you this, but I'm trying to break things to you easily."

"That's not a funny joke." Lucian didn't laugh. Nathan tried to sit up and look down his body, but it was too much for him. "What happened to my body? I think you've done something to me. Demi did this, didn't she? She had them hurt me so that I'll leave her alone. Well, it won't work."

"And there is the real Nathan." He didn't understand that, but Demi spoke, and both him and Lucian turned to look at her. She did look tired, but she'd hurt him, and he was going to make her pay.

"I was just telling him about the loss of his leg."

"You didn't take care of yourself, and they had to remove it before a clot that was there broke from the ones in your leg and killed you." He told Demi that she lied. "Why would I do something like that when you can fucking look down at yourself and see that I'm not?"

He tried again to look, and this time Lucian helped him. There was blood on the sheets, and he couldn't see his foot sticking up like the other one was. Then he looked at the rest

141

of his body. He was bleeding through the sheets at his belly too. Nathan looked at Demi, terrified out of his mind over what she'd done to him.

"I've done nothing, Nathan. You knew that this could happen when you decided to eat several hundred dollars' worth of candy and alcohol at the hotel. Then there was before. You ate whatever you could shovel into your mouth, and now you're paying the price." He told her again that she lied. "What do I have to do to get you to believe that your leg, from the knee down, is gone? Help you walk? That won't help you at all. You'll just fall on your fat ass. Listen to me, you fucking moron. You're fucking going to die if you don't start taking responsibility for yourself and pay attention to your body."

He'd made her cry. Glancing at Lucian, he wondered if he would blame him for this. Demi had done all this to him, and now she was getting upset. Nathan said her name and she looked at him. For a moment, just a short one, he could see her pain, just as he had when she'd been younger, and he'd beaten her. But he shoved those feelings away when he thought of Astrid.

"Where is my sister? The one that never did a thing to me but be my friend?" Demi looked at Lucian, then at him. "What? Did you do something to her too? You fucking bitch. I swear, when I'm out of here, I'm going to murder you."

"She's gone." He asked where she'd gone. "She's dead, Nathan. Four days ago. Astrid went into a bank with a gun and tried to rob it. The police had no choice but to kill her or be killed."

"No. Why must you keep lying to me, Demi? What have I ever done to you that would make you say things like this about my only sister?" He looked at Lucian when he made a low sound. "You were nothing to me. Nor Astrid. You're just doing this to be mean and cruel, when you know that you've cheated us out of everything all along. Go away. I don't want to ever see you again. Send my sister in too."

Nathan could see Demi crying, but it didn't matter to him. She wasn't nice. He'd never done a thing to her that would make her want to lie so cruelly to him.

Just before the door shut on them, Demi came back. He knew it — it was all a great big lie.

"Nathan, I'll pay the bills until you're out of the hospital. I know that you think that I owe you something, but I'm finished with you. There will be nothing for you from now on. And if you come near me or mine, I will have you arrested. This time I will press charges too. While you laid there, suffering and in pain, all I could think about was that you might have a change of heart, that you might just be able to make room for me in yours. But I can see now that not only was I a fool for thinking that, but also one for trying to be a good sister all along." Nathan wanted to scream at her that she'd never been anything to him or his sister. "I guess that all I've been to you, ever, is someone you could knock around and steal from when you thought I had anything. I'm so sorry. Sorry that you'll never know my children, that you'll never know my heart, and most importantly, you'll never understand what it is to truly be loved by someone and to love them back. Goodbye, Nathan. I won't wish you good will. You've used that all up."

After she was gone, he sat up again in the bed. The blood was worse now. He didn't know how she'd made his foot so he'd not be able to see it, but he'd get to the bottom of it. Or

Astrid would. Leaning back on the bed, he used the button on the side to call the nurse. When she came in, he asked for Astrid.

"I'm sorry, Mr. Morgan. We were told that you knew that she'd passed away. Her funeral was just yesterday. Would you like for me to bring you a copy of the paper to read about it?" He laughed, wondering at the lengths someone would go to to make his heart hurt. He told her that would be nice. "I'll be in after I finish up my rounds. Do you need anything?"

"I've already told you. Don't you listen? I want my sister. Call Astrid up and tell her that this is going on too long. And to bring me something to eat." The nurse told him that he was on a diet, a very strict one. "No. I'm not going to be on a diet just yet. If you can see your way to help me out, I'm sure that Demi will pay you. I'd like a pie. Not a single slice of one, but a whole pie and ice cream. I've a craving something terrible for one."

Nathan made a mental list of things that he wanted from Astrid. She'd have money, he supposed. She had been able to rob a bank. He wished he could have seen her in action. Maybe if he'd not gotten so sick, he might have gone to help her. So long as he didn't have to run. Running wasn't something that he was any good at anymore.

His mind skittered over something that was said to him — something to do with his legs — but he let it go. There wasn't anything that Demi said that he'd believe. And the fact that she'd gotten his nurse to go along with her showed just what sort of mean nasty person she was. And she was a thief, taking their money and home.

Closing his eyes, he waited for his nurse to return. His mind was all over the place with things that he wanted. His pie still hadn't come, but Nathan was all right with that. He decided that he wasn't all that hungry anyway. And he hurt too. Again, his mind moved quickly over why he might not be feeling up to things, but like before, he simply let it go.

Before he knew it, he was waking up again. The newspaper was lying on his little table. It was difficult to get the thing close to him—his belly was really beginning to hurt now. Nathan wondered briefly if he'd eaten something rotten and picked up the paper to read what his sister had done to rob a bank. Boy, he thought, she sure was a pistol.

The lights were difficult to get to come on. A voice somewhere in the room asked if he needed something, and he said that he was looking for the light. The voice said that he'd be in in a few minutes, it was time to change his dressing.

"But I'm not terribly hungry." The man said nothing, only that he'd be in soon with something for pain. "All right. I am hurting a great deal. Perhaps you can tell me what happened while you're at it. Did I eat something bad?"

He waited for a few more minutes, and finally the man—he said his name was Michael—came in. There was a tray with him that was covered with a cloth, and Nathan thought it was his pie. Before he could tell him that he no longer wanted it, Michael pulled the cover off and Nathan could see that it was bandages and stuff.

"I'm going to give you something for pain in your IV, Mr. Morgan. That way when I pull off the bandages, you won't hurt as badly." He asked about the pie. "According to your chart, you're no longer allowed anything sweet. And you have to start eating very low carb meals all the time."

"Why?" He repeated what Demi had told him. That because he'd not taken care of his diabetes, he'd gotten a blood clot on his leg that had festered, and the leg had to be removed. "I don't understand. If you removed the blood clot, what does that have to do with me having a piece of pie? This is all Demi's doing, isn't it? She paid you to tell me these things, didn't she? And where is Astrid? She should be here with me. I'm her brother."

"I'm sorry, sir, but Ms. Morgan is dead. You've been told that several times."

The man pulled the sheet off his leg and had him look at it. Nathan felt his belly, that was already hurting, start to swim, and his head felt like it was coming off again.

He could hear Michael saying his name, over and over, but he just couldn't get himself to answer. His leg was gone. Demi had taken his leg. Why would she do that? To sell? She was a horrible person. A very horrible person.

~*~

Lucian was worried about Demi. She was working like she normally did, going over reports and making sure that things were up on the stocks. But he could tell that she was hurting. And there wasn't much he could do to make it better.

"Your brother, Ian, did I tell you that he's working on my computer things for the restaurant we own?" Lucian told her that she had. "I thought so. Anyway, I've closed it up for a few days. It's something that I do to all the restaurants that we own—you might want to know that too. It's on that calendar that we share."

"I saw that. Thank you for making it so I can keep up. I have to tell you, love, I never knew that it was so exhausting to be wealthy." She laughed, and he was glad to hear it sounded normal. "Why do you close up?"

"Oh, because there are deep fryers in some of them that

need to have the screens cleaned once every six months. I could get by with just once a year, but then I'd have a bigger build up, and I would hate that." He nodded, understanding that from working fast food in high school. "The walk ins are also cleaned out and checked for any leaks or troubles. Painting is done in the dining area, and the carpets are cleaned or replaced at that time as well." She smiled at him. "Once when we did this, a while ago, we were cleaning the walk in and found some used condoms. The most disgusting thing I've ever heard. I shut the place down and had the entire walk in replaced. I still couldn't eat there."

"I'm sure that I wouldn't have been able to either. What else have you found?" She told him a few other things — nothing as bad as the condoms, however. "The cameras; do you have those in all the restaurants now?"

"Most everywhere we own, there is some kind of camera security system in place. It's not just for me keeping an eye on things, like the one I'm having trouble with, but also the people there. We have a security team that monitors them and keeps everyone out of trouble. You'd be surprised how much goes on that a camera can catch."

"You are not going to believe this." Ian came into the room. He was laughing and holding a sheet of paper. "Pull up the security camera on the Rusted Nail. You aren't going to believe this."

As she pulled up the camera on her computer, he stepped behind her. Ian asked Lucian through their link if she was all right, and he shrugged, but told him that she was doing better than he thought.

They both looked at the camera when she asked about focus. At first Lucian wasn't sure what he was looking at until

Ian moved the mouse. And suddenly it was crystal clear that someone was loading up a grocery cart full of things from the walk-in.

"At first I wasn't sure what he was doing. I knew that this was the last day for the Nail to be open, so I thought he was gathering stuff to make a send-off meal. But then I saw him loading the things into his car. This is his third cart load. He won't get far, Demi. The police are waiting for him to leave before they arrest him."

The three of them watched as he struggled to get a side of beef off the shelf and into his cart. It kept falling over, the weight not quite right on the cart. They were having such a good time that he'd forgotten for a moment that this man was stealing from them.

"All right. I've seen enough. He's a moron of the first degree and thought for sure that he was sliding by me when I was in his office." She looked up at him. "I'm really all right. I hurt, I won't lie to you, about that, but I'm all right."

When Daniel got what he could out of the restaurant, he started away with the goods. The police were waiting for him as he drove around the parking lot to leave and he was arrested. No fanfare, but that was one less thing that they had to worry about. Ian thanked Demi and him for hiring him. It was the best job he'd ever had, he told them.

The two of them sat there for several minutes before she stood up. "I have to go and see a house. Would you like to come with me? I have it in my head that one of your brothers would like it once we turn it around. It's out of date in some areas." He said he'd love to go.

They were leaving the house when the phone rang. Telling him that she wasn't in the mood to talk to someone, he took the call for her. When he hung up, devasted about the news, he went to the car where she was waiting.

"Don't tell me." He said that he didn't have to, but she'd have to know sooner or later. "Yes, perhaps, but not right now. Let's just forget about life that has me all bogged down and see this house. I'm thinking Josiah will like this one. He told me once that he liked older homes, the kind where closets had to be added but it still had claw footed tubs. And he said that he would buy one if the kitchen was a cook's dream. Did you know that he loves to cook?"

"I did. This house, it has a nice kitchen then?" She said that she didn't know how nice it was, but according to their business realtor, it was huge. They pulled up in front of the house. Christ, it was huge.

The wrap around porch reminded him of his time in New Orleans. He'd spent a week there after graduation from high school. The color and people were wonderful, and he loved the long vines of flowers hanging from the upper floors of places.

They walked through the house together. Demi would point out things that needed to be fixed or replaced, while he pointed out the charm of the woodwork and the fireplace mantles. He thought it was funny that he was the romantic and she wasn't. She could be, he supposed, but in houses like this one, it was all business. Lucian loved that about her too.

"The dining room isn't very big. I'd push it out beyond the porch and put in lots of windows. Give the room the illusion of being larger. But if your brother wants it, he'll want larger. Then I'd just scrap this room and make an entire addition off the back, and this could be a large walk in pantry and laundry room, and freezer storage area." He loved that idea. "Also, if he does want to put in the larger room, it would be easy to blend it into this house, and no one would ever know that it wasn't built when the house was."

Lucian loved the way her mind worked. And he knew that if asked later what they'd talked about, she'd be able to tell someone verbatim what they'd said. The amount of work that needed to be done and how long it would take. Christ, she had the perfect head for business. She asked him what he'd found that needed work.

"I think you about covered it all. But I was thinking of the bannister. I think that it needs to be back dated. What I mean is, someone put in that ugly one, and I don't think it was original to the home. Do you?" They walked back into the main hall and looked at it. "No, I think this is made of pressed wood."

"It is. Good catch. And see the spindles? I never noticed it, but they don't all match. That would drive a person who likes detail nuts. Josiah is like that, I've noticed. His work area is always neat and cleaned up." Lucian had noticed that as well when he'd gone to see how his job was working out. All his pens faced the same way, and there wasn't a single water bottle mark on his desk. "Do you want to call your brother and see if he has time to come meet us here? I'm going to purchase it regardless of his decision."

"What will you do with it then?" She said she'd offer it to one of his other brothers. "Good, but I think that if Josiah doesn't want it, then he's having an off day. And if they don't want it?"

"Then we'll rent it out to people with families. Of course, we'll make sure we get a hefty deposit from them. Or even staff it and bring other businesses here to look around and let

them stay in this place. Full of that country charm and shit."
They both laughed. And he looked up the stairs again. "What
are you thinking, Lucian? I really want you to feel like you
can be a part of every decision we make concerning business
dealings. Life too."

"I know that. And I love you for it. But I'm just a poor
country boy at heart, and I'm terrified of spending money. I
know we have plenty. I'll get better, but it's taking me some
time to get used to it. Now you want to see someone getting
used to having money, you should see Mom. She's been
ordering people around for decades, and now she's happy to
be getting paid for it." They both laughed.

His mom had been recommended to the school board.
Demi had done it, wanting someone there that would get
matters taken care of. And as soon as she was there, the very
first day, Mom fired two people and hired four much needed
teachers. She had also been working on an after-school
program for children who were struggling to keep up. Lucian
thought she was doing a fantastic job.

"Your mom is the best. I do hope you know that." He said
he did. Mom told him that every day. "I've actually heard her
say that to one of you. But she is my hero. To have raised six
sons without much in the way of income and keeping you in
school — that had to take someone with a strong heart and a
brilliant mind. She's a pleasure to work with as well."

His mom had said the same thing about working with
Demi. And his dad couldn't say enough great things about
Lucian's wife. She was a little on the rough side, they both
had said, but she was good at making a point come across and
getting things done. That was what this town had needed for
a very long time.

Lucian called Josiah. He said that it was Thursday and he had started closing for half a day on that day. "It gives everyone here a day that they can make appointments and have family time, and it's a good day, right before the Saturday rush, to rest up. I'll be there in about an hour."

They sat outside, talking about what needed to be done here. There was a lot more that they wanted done, but they thought that if Josiah wanted the house, then he'd be able to make the decisions. Lucian could not wait for his brother to see the kitchen. He thought it was going to be the deciding factor for his brother.

Chapter 11

Josiah didn't want to get overly excited about the house. It was perfect. Other than the things that really needed to be updated and fixed, he loved it. But he could also see the things that Lucian was pointing out. Demi, for some reason, was staying back and not saying all that much. Josiah was afraid they were going to play good cop and bad cop on him and bully him into taking it. Not that it would take all that much bullying.

"The dining room is too small for our family if you do buy it. We were thinking that you could expand into the back yard and make it wide and long so that you could fit a nice sized table in it. Or several, depending on whether or not you wanted to find something old to put in there." Josiah glanced at Demi as Lucian talked about the room. "You could turn this into a large pantry, and have —"

"What's going on here?" Demi asked him what he meant. "I don't know. It's like you're this wilting housewife letting the big husband take care of things. That's so not like you.

153

Hell, that's not even close to being anything like my mom. What gives?"

"I could be if I wanted. Wilting, I mean. I don't care for it, but in a pinch, I could do it." Josiah said it was creepy coming from her. "Such a fast talker about a woman. No, I'm hoping that Lucian can talk you into purchasing this house. I'd just tell you to shut up, buy it, and we'll work out the details later. But I'm trying really hard not to seem like I'm forcing you into anything."

"I see." She asked him if he did. "No. I have the feeling that you're grooming Lucian for something."

"Sort of. He needs to learn to not only sell things, but himself too. How's he doing?" Josiah, lost in thought now, said that his brother could use some of her right to the point. "Sometimes it will take a softer approach to things. I can't do that. I'm not the soft type. Not that Lucian is, but he can talk someone into something while I just want to move on to the next thing by telling them that they're buying it. Understand?"

"Yes. I do. And I think I'd like to take a few lessons from you on that part of selling. While I can do the softer approach, I think that there are times when I need to be firmer." Demi told him what Jamie had said about his sales. "Our sales. We're working as a team, which is something that we were never able to do before."

"You're a good man, Josiah. And what about this house? Is it right for an up and coming dealership manager?" He wanted to be coy about it, but the house was just what he'd wanted. Instead of answering her, Josiah asked her how much it was. "How much the bank wants or how much I'm willing to pay for it?"

"There's a difference?" She said a huge one. "Okay, before

154

I answer that question—which I wouldn't even know how— tell me why you'd, I'm assuming, pay less for it. And tell me why the bank will want more. Please."

"The house has been sitting on the market for almost four years. The bank has someone come out once a month who mows but doesn't trim. He is to check on pipes, leaks that might have sprouted, as well as make sure that the furnace— which needs to be replaced—as well as the air conditioner— which also needs to be updated—are working. The kitchen, as you have noticed, is in need of a complete overhaul. I'd start from the walls and rip it to the studs." He could see that too. "The dining room, as Lucian pointed out, isn't nearly big enough for your family when they come over. Which I can assume they will. They love you guys, and love to be together. And the roof needs to be redone and in places replaced, as it looks a little lopsided on one side."

"Is that all?" She said that was just the things that would cost the most to fix. "And the cost to fix those things? It is more than the asking price of the house from the bank?"

"Yes. But you have a solid foundation here, plenty of yard and acreage too. If this house were fixed the way it should be, then you're talking about a house worth, in this area, about half a million dollars. In this area, now. But, when we are finished bringing businesses in, upgrading the three schools here and having some major high-end stores come in, you're talking over a million. I'd say in less than five years." Lucian asked if she was serious. "I never joke about money. Ever. It's not something that is funny to me."

"All right. I can't afford this house. Not and do the repairs as well. What sort of deal will you make me if we work together on this?" She smiled. "That's not as comforting as you might think, Demi. You look like a shark, if you want to know the truth."

"Good. That's what I go for when I'm in a meeting. But you will get the family discount. I will pay for the repairs and you can purchase the house. I will also make the deal on it for you. I think I can do a great deal better than the bank is asking right now." Josiah asked how much the bank wanted. "Just over four hundred thousand. But I can get them to come down. I promise you."

"They would have to come down a great deal for me to be able to afford that. I mean, I have a good paying job now, but not that good. Not yet anyway." Demi told him to let her handle this part for him. "All right. But the best price possible. Then how to I pay you back for the repairs and upgrades?"

"When you sell the house. Which I'm sure you won't want to after you see it. But if you do, then I get half of the upgrade price back." He asked what happened if he didn't sell. "Then we both break even. I have a brother-in-law close, and you have a lovely home. One you might one day fill with children."

"Yes, well, that day could be far, far away. All right. We'll work on this after you talk to the bank." She laughed, and Josiah realized that this had been a set up from the start, and it made him laugh as well. "You've talked to the bank already, haven't you?"

"Yes. They were very cooperative after I helped them with the other bank manager. And they said that they would do just about anything for me. When I pointed out that this house was clogging up their books, they were more than happy to let me take it off their hands." Softly, Josiah asked her how much they'd been helpful to her. "I got it for a steal—for nothing.

As I said, they were very happy with me, and since I was very willing to leave some of our money in the bank locally, they said that you can have it. All you need to do, Josiah, is go to the bank when you can and sign the paperwork. As soon as you do, the house is yours. And construction on it will begin tomorrow morning."

~*~

Lucian had never seen any of his brothers dance, much less a jig. And Josiah hugged them both several times before he sat down. He kept repeating over and over that he was a home owner. They were still laughing at him as they made their way out to the car. After Josiah pulled away, heading toward the bank, Demi turned to him.

"I've found my niece, the one that belonged to Astrid. So now both of them are in our care. And I found out how Astrid wasn't able to murder her child. By the way, they're both safe now, and we've set up a college fund for them both, as well as provided them with a check each month to help with expenses. Both sets of parents are strapped for money. Or they were." He asked her how it had been possible with her sister. "She was in rehab. I was told that she'd hit a parked car and had been found guilty of drunk driving—again. When she showed up to court for her sentencing drunk, the judge ordered her to go in. She was pregnant when she arrived, and the staff had to work very hard in keeping Astrid and her daughter safe. Astrid tried several times to fall down stairs, and anything else she could to rid herself of the child. The father was located and has been with the child since. Money was tight, but he was afraid to ask for money from the system for fear that Astrid would try and take Ashley from him. That's her name, Ashley Crosby. She just turned ten. Nathan's

157

little girl is Dana Morgan, and she's six. What happened? I'm assuming that Nathan has died."

"Yes. This morning. He was read the newspaper of the accounting of Astrid robbing the bank and how she was killed. The doctor told me that he'd taken it well at first, then he started screaming that you had tricked them. That you robbed them." She nodded. "I never read the paper's accounting, but is it that much different than what really happened?"

"Astrid went into the bank to try and take money out of my accounts. She didn't know that you were on them as yet, but she wanted her share. I'm not even sure how she thought that trying to get money from them was going to work in her favor." Lucian watched Demi as she stared out the window toward the house. "She was demanding they call me and have me meet her there. I was called, but never made it there before she drew her gun and fired at the ceiling. The police were there as well, called by a very smart teller who was on break, and when she fired, they fired back. She was dead long before she hit the floor."

"Do you feel like it was your fault?" She didn't answer him. "Demi, you had nothing to do with either of their deaths. You know that, don't you?"

"What I do know is that they would have taken and taken from us until we were broke. I know that they would never have stopped. There was always something else they needed, something more that they should have. In all the time that I lived at home, and even after I left, neither Nathan nor Astrid ever had a job. It was much easier for them to steal than it was for them to work for something." He nodded, knowing people just like them. "Why did someone read the paper to him? To be cruel?"

"No. Apparently your brother couldn't read well. They think, after the way he described it to the nurse, that he was dyslexic." She said that she'd not known that. "No, I didn't think you did. But there is more; are you ready for it?"

"Yes. And no." She looked at him. "When we're able to settle things up, get our life on an even place, I'd like to go away with you. To see the world, one of our homes at a time."

"Deal. Do you want me to give you the highlights, or all of the details I have?" He held her hands when she told him details, she was better with details. "After the article was read to him, he laid there for the longest time. The doctor had put someone on him to watch over him, but there was a COD in one of the nearby rooms. The nurse went there to assist. Nathan rolled himself out of the bed and onto the floor. There he used the blood from his wound to say that it was all your fault before he killed himself. He used the bed rail to break his own neck."

Demi was quiet on the way home. Lucian wasn't sure what to do now, or to say. But when they got home, she turned to him before they were able to get out of the car. After she kissed him lightly on the mouth, he asked her if she was all right.

"I will be. Now anyway. I've lost all my biological family in a matter of months, and I'm not at all sure how I should feel about that, to be honest. But I do want something from you." He told her anything. "I want us to tell our children every day that we love them. That we don't spoil them with money even though we can. I don't want them to grow up thinking that anything and everything is owed to them. They'll work for what they want, and work harder for their grades. They'll learn the family business too. Just as you're doing now."

159

"I like that idea. And we need to set up college funds for them too. Ones that will help them through college, but perhaps not pay for parties and shit." She nodded. "Also, while we're on the subject, I'd like to go to college. I mean, I need to go to college to learn how to manage a business, so that I, too, have to earn my keep."

"Excellent idea. I love it. And we should make it so that any of your family that wishes to go back, to— Why are you shaking your head no? Don't you want them to go to college?" He nodded, but said they could earn their way, just as he did. "And just how did you earn your education?"

"I'm having a baby with you." She smiled at him. "There's my girl. How about we go in, take care of whatever has to be taken care of, and go up to bed. I don't know about you, but this being rich shit is tiring."

"Yes, I'm sure you just wore yourself out too. I guess you're not in the mood for sex then?" He wiggled his brows at her. "I see. Well, if I have to suffer though it with you, then I will."

They were both laughing when they entered the house. Lucian surely did love this woman. And having a baby with her was just like having his cake and the icing too. Or something like that.

~*~

Doctor Walker watched the young woman. She'd been in his care for nearly six years now, and there had been no improvement at all in her state of mind. He had to either send her to a nursing home soon, or to a home that would keep her as unknown and as safe as he'd done. Judson was sure that someone somewhere would find her here, and that just wouldn't do—not in a constant catatonic state like she had been in. The poor girl had suffered like no one else ever had.

He remembered the day that she'd been brought to his facility. It had been a cold day in December — the day after Christmas, as a matter of fact. Meadow had been in the hospital before coming here, her wounds too great to think that she was even going to live. But she had, defying all odds against her.

The police and everyone else that had had anything to do with her trial had said that she'd brutally murdered her entire family, the staff, as well as the family dog. But Meadow had been found unfit to stand trial, her state of mind making it so that she couldn't answer their questions or help figure out what exactly had happened that day, if she wasn't the one that had killed them all.

According to teachers, as well as neighbors, Meadow had been a fun, loving sixteen-year-old. She'd just gotten her driver's license the day before. She didn't have anyone that disliked her, nor did she have any boyfriends. And certainly, no lovers.

The police had gone to the home of the Springs, a very prominent family in their hometown, to see where the father was. He'd been scheduled to chair a meeting, one that would start the process of next year's holiday celebration. When they found the door open, it was called in as a simple breaking and entering. But it was worse. So much worse.

"Judson, it's that newspaper man again. He is asking the delivery people if he can sneak in and get a picture of the young woman. I have had him run off several times, but he just won't give up." His nurse of nearly forty years, and his wife of just a little less — Margaret — looked in the direction that he'd been looking. "She's such a delicate thing, isn't she?

161

I can't imagine why anyone in the world would think that she had the ability to do such brutality to someone, especially her own family. Not like they said had happened."

Not everyone knew the entire story. He did. He had been the doctor on call that day for the police. Acting coroner as well. Going into the house, knowing that it was going to be messy, he wasn't prepared for what he'd seen. No one was, apparently, as there were several hardened police officers in the bushes losing their breakfast.

After telling his wife to run the newspaper man off then call the police, Judson headed to his office. There he reached into his lower drawer and pulled out the false bottom. Only his wife knew that it was there, the file that he'd put together just after Meadow had come to his facility. Along with the pictures that he'd taken the day of the murders.

The butler had answered the door, from what they could tell. His body had been mutilated beyond knowing if he was male or female, except for the uniform that he wore. Blood was sprayed from the front door all the way up ten of the stairs in the house. After whoever had killed him with a single bullet to the heart, they had finished up by taking an axe to his face and chest. Then they moved through the house to the kitchen. The rest of the staff was there, as it was still early yet.

Both the upstairs maids, as well as the cook and gardener, had been murdered in the kitchen. Their bodies not as unrecognizable as the butler's, but almost as bad. The murderer had taken his time with the butler but seemed rushed with the other staff. The dog, a new puppy for Meadow's brother, had been found with his neck broken, and his head had been split by tearing his mouth open until bones were shattered.

Flipping through the pictures of the man and his wife, he

went to the ones of the children. Mostly he was focused on Meadow and her brother. She had tried to save the little boy. To him it was as obvious as the nose on his face.

They were found in his bed. The six-year-old had been murdered too, his small body not large enough for the damage that had been done to it. There was nothing left of his face, nothing of his chest. And in her effort to save him, Meadow had been cut badly, almost fatally.

Covered in her brother's blood, the axe had nearly taken her hand off; her blood loss was what had nearly killed her. Her head had been cut like the others, but to this day, Judson believed that the murderer had been nearly caught. By someone coming to the door? The police, perhaps?

It would be unknown until Meadow was able to tell them. Nothing was final until she was able to point her finger at someone and say they had done this horrific crime. For as long as he lived, Judson would never believe that a child like Meadow had been would ever have been able to do such a thing.

Right now, he had to work on getting Meadow to a facility to hide her away again. With that idiot news reporter coming around now, he would eventually find a way in. Or worse yet, take her out of here to question her himself. It had happened before.

When Meadow had been in the hospital, a person came in saying that he was her uncle—some distant one that only had just heard about the deaths. He hadn't been there—Judson might have been a little more on his toes by asking for identification. But as it was, the man got all the way to the front of the hospital, with her unconscious, before someone thought that he might not have been who he said he was.

They had transferred her to his facility almost a week later, when Meadow could be moved without causing any wounds to open again.

"Judson, come here please." His wife's voice sounded strained. He hurriedly put his things away and rushed to see what was happening. Margaret pointed in the direction of where Meadow was sitting. "See it?"

"No, I'm sorry love, I don't—" Then it hit him. She was sitting there with her head tilted back, smiling. "She is enjoying the sunlight. Have you ever seen her do that before?"

"No. I stared at her just like you did and knew there was something different about her, but not what it was until I saw the smile. She's smiling, Judson."

For the last two years they'd been keeping her progress unknown to anyone but the two of them. They had nursing staff, of course. But since they owned several of this sort of home for people, they continued to rotate them in and out so that no one knew too much about any one patient. That was the way the people who had hired them liked it. Privacy was a huge thing. But they had stopped giving information even to her attorney.

Margaret was the first person to have grown a dislike to the man. She called him oily. He hadn't had any feelings for him one way or the other. But then once, when he'd come to see them about some other matter, he asked if they had any naked pictures of Meadow.

"Why would we have those? She wears clothing while she's here." He asked if she took a shower or not. "Of course she does. We don't allow our patients to be unclean. What sort of question is that?"

"I just asked. You don't have to get your binders in a knot.

Christ."

After that the attorney, Lee Shiloh, didn't come by any more. The checks that they were getting came in the mail now. But he did want progress reports, every week. And they'd been saying the same thing all along—no change. And would continue to say that even after today.

"We'll have to get her moved, and soon." Margaret said that she agreed. "I'll look around for an out of the way nursing home and arrange to have her sent there. The only person we have to contact is her doctor."

Doctor of Behavioral Health Max Little had been by to see the young woman regularly. He also brought her a birthday card and gift each year, and made sure that she had chocolate, something they had discovered, soon after he started bringing the confection, that Meadow didn't care for. Doctor Little had said to give it to the staff or other patients, as his wife was the one that had picked it out year after year. And even after Mrs. Little passed away, Doctor Little still brought the candy. It was habit now, he supposed.

Making a call to the doctor, he asked about the sunlight in her face. Then he questioned how she might make a trip so that no one knew it was her, or even noticed a person leaving the building. Judson told him about both the newspaper man and the attorney.

"I think she'd be all right with it. So long as she's not tied down on a bed. That frightens her something terrible." They both knew why. She'd been tied up when they'd brought her into the hospital, and she had only wanted her brother with her. "Also, if you know of a nice place that she could go, that would be good too. My wife and I will certainly miss her, but I think that in light of recent events, we have to get her out of here."

"Yes, I agree. And as a matter of fact, I do know of a place. It's in Ohio where all this began, as you know. I just made a trip that way a couple of weeks ago for their grand reopening of their facility. Nice place, Judson. You might even travel with Meadow so that you can have a look around. Take the missus and make a vacation of it for a few days. I'm sure that we can figure out a billing so that it's all taken from the estate. Plus, she might need someone there that she knows. You never know about patients like Meadow, and what their reactions might be."

"Yes, I remember when she was brought here. It was a mess until we found her little stuffed dog." She had outgrown the dog now, but he'd kept it. If she remembered something, it might help her to have something of her brother's. That's who they figured it belonged to. "I'll start packing up her things now. If you could see if they have the room and if they can accommodate her things, that would be wonderful."

"You just pack her up. I'll call them right now to see what sort of arrangements I can make with them. It's a very lovely place. From my understanding, the entire town is getting a makeover."

They closed the connection and he went to see who was left on staff. Meadow would be moved in the darkness of night. Her things would be packed up by him and Margaret, and by the next shift change, there would be no trace of the young woman. That was the way it had to be done. There was still a great deal of —

"Margaret, what's the date?" She had to look on her cell phone. "Oh my. That's why we're having that reporter around. The anniversary is coming up soon. They'll want to get pictures of her and make up some sort of story like they have spoken to her. I'll have to remind Max of that when he calls us later."

He did call back later, and after talking about the home in Ohio, he said that tonight would be the best time. As much as he hated to sedate her, after her progress from today, they knew that would be the only way to slip her into a body bag — to look as if someone had died — and ship her out. It was the only way, and the safest way for her to be moved.

"Margaret, we're going to go out tonight too. Head to Ohio to be with Meadow when she wakes up." She thought that was a good idea. "We don't have anyone here but her at the moment, and all the staff is on to other places as of the end of the shift tonight at eleven. We won't even be missed for a few days. The cleaning crew comes in tomorrow, and by then, the place will be empty. Of everything."

"All right. I'll pack us up an overnight bag. Also, we should act a little teary for her leaving us if we want that newspaper jerk to believe that she has passed away." He thought that a splendid idea. "I have them on occasion. We'll take the flight out then?"

"Yes, it's being arranged for us." She nodded, and after she left him to go pack, he started gathering everything up that was related to Meadow. There wouldn't even be a scrap of paper left behind, and Max was going to see to Meadow being loaded himself.

Judson just hoped that things went well for her — that she'd continue to want to have the sun on her face, and that she smiled once in a while. At this point in her life, it was more than they could have hoped for.

Chapter 12

Lucian was finished setting up his office. He also had a specialized room at the house where he could go and do homework. Since he'd enrolled in his first class, taking it easy his first year, things had begun to fall into a normal place for him. It was like everything that he needed to have done was running along smoothly for a change. When Josiah entered the office, he showed him around. But Lucian could tell that he was distracted.

"I think perhaps Demi and I are going to have fifty kids in our lifetime. We're going to name them with numbers. You know, one, two, three. That way we won't have to come up with a new name each time." Josiah said that was nice. "Yes, I thought you'd say that. We're also having a custom car made. It'll have layers on it so that we only have to push a button and the top opens up to make more seating. But the police have to escort us everywhere, because—"

"Do you think she's coming?" He asked him who. "My mate, you fucking moron. Weren't you listening to me?"

169

"Apparently neither one of us were listening to each other. No, I don't have any idea if she's coming or not." Josiah picked up the pencil holder that had come with Lucian's office set. He was still trying to figure out if he used pens in it, would it be renamed. Josiah said his name. "I don't understand why you're obviously upset about this."

"Is that why you talked me into buying that house?" Lucian just sat on the corner of his desk and waited. "I know you didn't do that, but I have to blame someone. Did you know that it cost nearly four thousand dollars to tear out a room and put up in another one? Then there is the electrical work. Plumbing has to be redone, even though I have no idea why they'd think that I'd want water in the dining room." He told him why. "Oh. Okay, I can see having water outside and it running through that room. But Christ, Lucian, it's fucking making me crazy spending all this money."

"Okay, let me show you something, and I had to learn this way as well. I'm going to show you mine and Demi's accounts." Josiah said not to do that. "I promise you, Josiah, you'll understand if I show you."

Demi came in the office just as he was pulling up their accounts. Lucian told her what was going on, and she sat in the chair that he'd just unwrapped. Demi smiled at Josiah and had him sit in the other chair that hadn't been unwrapped as yet.

"I was wondering how long it would be before you started to feel the pressure of spending money on something. It's a hard lesson to realize, isn't it?" Josiah pointed out that she'd grown up with money. "No, I didn't. My grandma had money. We didn't. The only reason that we had food was because of my grandma. And the first year that I was out on my own, I was eating crackers a great deal, and water. Nothing else until I started making money. Now…well, I worry about it, but not like I did before."

Josiah came around to Lucian's side of the desk when he called to him. He watched his brother's face as he looked at the three accounts that he'd pulled up. One of them was their bank account, the second was their stocks, and the third was their investment in a very large computer company. Josiah asked why the numbers were changing all the time.

"The investment company will fluctuate up and down over the course of the day. But if you notice, it never goes below the number it was at first. It'll climb up ten points then lower by four, then go up by seven. It's ever changing, but always making money. The computer company is in a good place now." Demi came around the desk as she continued to explain. "We just expanded to another state, and that took a hit on its bottom line. But as you can see, it's rebounded quickly and well. I'm very happy with that one. The bank account can only hold so much money. The reason that it goes up over that limit then back down is because the money that hits over the account amount is funneled to four separate accounts. The same thing is there. Once it gets to a limit, it's funneled again."

"How do you keep track of all this?" Demi had Lucian pull up the program that had astonished him. "What is that? And are those numbers right?"

"That is where at the end of the day, each and every day, I go in and put in what we made, what we lost, and how many other investments we made into each company." Lucian scrolled through the ledger. "Lucian is getting the hang of doing it. It takes me about an hour now because I know just where everything is. But he's getting it down too."

"Yes, with plenty of notes, and going back over what I've done several times to make sure that I'm not messing the numbers up. It's a lot of money we have. And I do have to keep reminding myself that this is our money, mine and Demi's. Josiah, if you need more or if it would make you feel better, I can give you a contract on what we're doing. But as she said, and she's right, we don't care if you ever get around to paying us back. As you can see, we don't need the money coming in from family."

Josiah sat down. He did look a good deal less stressed, but he didn't say much. Lucian turned to Demi. He knew where she'd been, and he was almost afraid to mention it in front of Josiah. He would think they were setting him up. But all they were doing was helping out the nursing home in town.

"She arrived about an hour ago. They have her room set up just like it had been. And the doctor that came with her approves. He said that her doctor would be by in a few days to make sure that she didn't need anything." Lucian nodded. "I'm also going to go over her paperwork from the trial, as well as her medical records. I don't have a great deal of experience with the medical stuff, but I can get someone to help me."

"I remember that case." Demi said that she did as well. "I guess the family murder was grisly. I remember reading that the entire household was murdered, including the dog."

"Yes. I'm just curious why they thought this girl could have done it. She was only sixteen then, and a good kid." Josiah asked how the dog was killed. "I guess, from what I've seen so far in the reports, his mouth was ripped open all the way back to his skull. Why do you ask?"

"She's human, I'm assuming, this little girl." Neither

of them corrected him about her being nearly twenty-five. "Then she couldn't have done it. A human, unless in full rage, would not have been able to tear open an animal's mouth. And I did get that she's an adult; just trying to equate her with the murders."

"Also, while you're in the mood to help me, it says that she wasn't trying to protect her brother but had hurt herself with the axe she'd been using on him and nearly bled to death. They never explain how she had so many marks on her body, nor the fact that she was hit from behind with the same axe." Josiah asked if they'd found any fingerprints. He still hadn't moved from the chair, nor had he looked at either of them. "Yes, plenty. They'd had a party the night before. It had started raining and everyone came into the house. They were everywhere. Also, and this one I find sort of funny. They said that Meadow knew the killer; that she'd let them in after everyone was in bed."

"They never left." Lucian looked at Demi and she smiled. Josiah looked at the two of them. "You've thought of that already."

"Yes, I had. But apparently, it's not possible to have happened. At least according to the police. I've seen that house. It's a big place, bigger than yours. And it sets back off the main road. You do remember that it happened not far from here, don't you? Like the next town over?" Lucian said he'd forgotten where it had happened. "Yes, that's why they're bringing her here. To hide out from that reporter and to see if the town sparks some memories. Because why would anyone think that they'd bring her back to the scene of the crime, so to speak, after all this time?"

"Why hide her out at all?" Demi explained to Josiah just

as it had been explained to her. "I see. I guess that would be hard on people that might have known the family. Having no idea who might have killed those people and why. I'm assuming that nothing was ever resolved."

"No, nothing. She was found to be unfit to stand trial. She hasn't spoken a word, nor done anything but wheel herself around in her chair. She has some issues with her arm, the one that had nearly been severed that day." Josiah asked Demi if she'd seen her. "No. They don't let anyone around her. As far as the place she's staying, all they know is that her name is Jane Doe, and that she has been in a horrific accident. I don't know what that would cover, honestly. I mean, has she a lot of scars that make it so no one would know her anyway? Whatever the reason, we're to make sure that she's safe, and that if anyone asks about her, we're to say nothing, but call the two doctors that have put her here."

Josiah sat there for a few more minutes while Lucian and Demi talked about the upcoming auction for things the city had collected over the years. It was brought to Demi's attention that they didn't have any idea who to contact about it. And after the paperwork was cleared to sell it off for a profit and get rid of the junk that was there, they decided to have it next weekend. Josiah cleared his throat and Lucian could see that he'd come to a decision.

"I'd like for you two to help me with my home. I'm not just overwhelmed, but I haven't a clue how to go about getting contractors to actually come in and do the work past getting estimates. I've tried getting reviews on a couple of them, but that hit a dead end too. I had no idea that you had to pay money to get into those sites." Demi told him that she already had a membership to most of them, but she'd help him. "Not just with that, its carpet colors and paint on the walls. As I said, I'm overwhelmed by the amount of questions that they will have for me from the list that I was given when I talked to one of the contractors. I will even have to tell them the color of cabinets and such. I haven't any idea on that."

"All right. We can do that for you." She smiled at his brother as Demi continued. "You really are doing a great job, Josiah. I didn't know how long it would take you, what with working full time and helping your dad move furniture and things around in their new home. You are a very smart man too. Jamie called me again last night and told me that he's going to be sending a few of his low performing managers to you so you can show them what you've done in such a short time. Did he tell you that he has employees at dealerships begging to be transferred to your base of operations?"

"He did. I'm not sure I believe him or not, but it felt really good." Josiah stood up. "Speaking of which, I have to get back to work. I'm half day tomorrow, so if you want to have me sign any paperwork, let me know. I can't thank you enough for helping me. Both of you. The house will look great, I know it will."

When Josiah left them, Demi sat on Lucian's lap facing him. She had had a hard morning, he knew that. And when she laid her head on his shoulder, it was all he could do not to run off with her and hide away.

"How about we do this? I hide in the woods. I know that you can find me easily enough, but if you give me some perks, I'll give you some." He asked her what sort of perks. "I don't know. You find me, I take something off. Then when I'm naked, you can fuck me as yourself, and then we'll lay by the pond back there and pretend that nothing is wrong with the world."

"Something else happen?" She nodded, then shook her head. "All right, love. We can do that. I'd love to chase you down as my bear. I'm assuming that's what you were talking about?"

"Yes. Sorry. It's been a weird and very long morning." Lucian said he was sorry. "It's all right. What I wanted isn't what I'm going to get in this deal with the city. It's not bad, just not what I wanted. But let's not talk about that now. I'm going in the yard."

He watched her go. She wasn't running, but he could see that her step was getting lighter as she made her way to the tree line. And when she got there, turned, and flipped him off, Lucian stood up, laughing. Demi was going to pay for that, he thought. And he'd win, too.

~*~

The woods were darker than she'd thought they'd be this late in the year. Demi assumed that with the leaves falling off the big trees, the sunlight would be better. She heard Lucian growl before he got to her, and they both went tumbling head over ass when he bumped her from behind.

"Not fair, you shithead." Demi ran her fingers over his soft fur. "Who would have thought that something so large and petrifying could be so soft and cuddly when you got really close? Of course, there are big teeth as well, but I love the way you feel under my hands."

It's my big brown eyes that do that for people. She laughed and hit him on the shoulder, standing up to run. *Excuse me? I caught you. You have to take something off. And not the shoes. I don't want you stepping on something sharp out here and ruining all our fun.*

176

"Your fun, you mean." She took off her shirt and tossed it at the big black bear. "I cannot wait to run with you. I'm glad that we asked your mom first before we started to change me. I don't know what I'd do if something happened to little cub."

She took off again and ran along the water, splashing the cold stuff up her legs and wetting her jeans. Demi thought to throw him off her scent, then she leapt up on the other side of the little waterway. There was a stand of deer just beyond her.

I see them. They didn't need to speak aloud anymore. Just with a thought she could talk to Lucian. She could feel his comfort when she needed it, and when she was happy, he felt that as well. *They come out nearly every night. Ian and I put out some hay for them, as well as some salt. I hope you don't mind.*

"No, I'm glad to see them here. Yesterday when I was on the phone in the office, I saw a pair of fox playing with their little kit. He was a very curious little guy. Nearly came all the way to the house but stopped. What else might we find out here?"

Well, I have seen, in my runs with my brothers, that there are some rabbits out there. A couple of burrows of them, so watch where you walk. Some mink too. But I think that's because no one will hunt them there. She asked if anything was endangered. *Not that I know of, but then I didn't think to look.*

"Grandma would never let anyone rake the leaves up on the estate. She said that we did more harm than good, and if you wanted your yard to be spotless then cut down all your trees and enjoy the boiling sun on your house. She didn't suffer fools well." Lucian said that she was like that too. "Yes, well, thank you. Even if you didn't mean it as a compliment."

I did. Something startled the deer and she turned to find Lucian. He was there, where she'd entered the waterway, sitting on his butt. He looked so much like a real bear that she asked if it was really him. *It's me, love. So you know, I can smell a stranger has been out here. We might want to be careful about that from now on.*

"I can do that." She started taking off her clothing. "I've decided that the grass looks really soft there. Provided that there isn't a great deal of deer poop. Why don't you make love to me here, and then later in the bed?"

I can do that. He shifted, his body becoming all man. His cock, hard and stiff, reminded her of a sword that he would carry. "I want you, love. More and more every day."

"And I want you, Lucian."

He met her at the side of the water. Lucian picked her up in his arms and carried her to where the deer had been. After looking around, he laid her down. At this moment Demi didn't care if she was laying in a pile of shit—she just wanted this man inside of her.

Demi loved when he touched her. His hands, softening up from not doing such hard work anymore, felt good on her overheated body. She realized that he wasn't so much touching her as he was marking her. His fingers would make her skin heated, like he'd put a branding iron to her, before he'd move to the next place on her body.

Lucian was very good at making love. He made her feel sexy, special, and beloved. There wasn't a time that he took her that he made her feel rushed, like he'd rather not be with her. Men in her past would be out to please themselves rather than her. It was like they were hurrying through sex so that they could move on to the next conquest. Men were very odd—most were anyway.

"Your breasts are fuller, have you noticed that?" She

shook her head, unable to make anything squeeze past the muscles in her throat. "And your nipples are so pink. I delight in tasting them. You are so beautiful, Demi. And I don't know what I'd have done had you not found me."

She kissed him, making up for the fact that she that speaking was impossible. He slid deep inside of her. Her body responded by flushing hotly, her pussy seeming to soak more. And when he began to move, his big body taking her over the top, she cried out his name several times before he kissed her again.

"Come for me, Demi. I want to feel you milk me." She nodded, wanting to please him in any way that she could. "That's it, baby. I can feel it, I can feel you rising up for me."

When she came, he bit down on her throat. It wasn't painful, but she did come harder the second time, then the third time, when he lifted her ass up, pulling her body to his so close that they looked like they were one. And when he dug his nails into her flesh, his claws biting into her as well, he cried out, his body bent back as he growled louder than she'd ever heard him do before.

Lucian dropped on top of her. She held him there. His hot skin felt wonderful under her fingers. And when he lifted just his head, she smiled at him and told Lucian how much she loved him.

"I love you as well. You are the world to—"

He stopped talking and stiffened. She did as well, knowing that something or someone was out there. Through their link, without moving, he told her to not move. To pretend like nothing was wrong.

Should I be worried? He didn't answer her as he moved off her, rolling to his back, bringing her with him. She thought that was scarier than him telling her she should be worried. *Lucian, you're scaring the shit out of me, and I'm fucking naked. If this is a joke, I'm not finding it very funny.*

I want you to roll to your back, then your belly. I'm going to roll the other way but come up as my bear. You stay here. I don't know what's out there, nor do I have any idea what they might have with them. She asked if he meant a gun. *Yes. Or something like that.*

The bullet zipped over her head. Before she could move, to worry about how close that had been, Lucian was his bear and no longer looked cuddly and soft. He was a fucking monster going after someone that had tried to hurt them.

Demi heard the screams, knowing that it wouldn't be Lucian; bears didn't scream, she told her rattled mind. Demi lifted her head just enough to see where he'd gone. She wished in that moment that she'd not—the blood was everywhere. The man that had shot at them was flying backward in the air, with his arm holding the gun dangling precariously from his body.

Laying her head back down, she counted to ten before she looked again. They were still fighting, and she laid her head back to the soft earth. That's when it occurred to her that it was more than one person—it was several.

She heard the stick snap as she was lifting her head again. The man apparently hadn't seen her, or he thought of her as no threat. Whatever, when he started to step where her head was, she grabbed his leg and shoved it upward, knocking him back. The rifle went off, the round in it flying up in the air, startling birds. Not waiting for him to get up or to aim at her this time, she jerked the rifle from him and bashed him in the head with it. She was ready to hit him a second time when the gun was jerked from her from behind.

Demi had learned hand to hand combat. So when she turned, she grabbed the man behind her and socked him in the face. Blood sprayed over her from his lips, and she knocked her forehead into the man's nose, causing him to drop like a rock. Demi dropped too, her legs weak with the use of adrenalin.

"Are you all right?" Demi looked behind her and a towel hit her in the face. "Go on now, honey, you go and wash up in that creek. The boys are coming too. I was just the closest one. My goodness, though, you had it all taken care of before I could shift and help you out. I don't think I'd be one to sneak up on you ever again. You sure do—"

"Alden. I'm all right." He nodded and looked away when she stood up to go to the waterway. Stopping, she looked for Lucian. "Where is he? Lucian, where did he go with that other group of men?"

"He's up the creek a bit. Got himself a little hurt. Nothing that won't be gone when he shifts, but he was more worried about you than getting himself cleaned up. I told him that I had you." Sitting in the water, she began splashing the cold liquid all over her face before scrubbing her arms and legs. "You are all right, aren't you, love? I was sure scared out of my mind when Lucian told us that someone was in the forest. Never would have believed that seven of them got by us."

"Did anyone check the guard house?" Alden said he'd not thought of that but would send one of the boys. "I have two men down there. I hope they're all right."

Demi was wrapping the towel around her just as Lucian came to where they were. He wasn't hurt—just a few scrapes and bumps on his face—but he looked good. Going to him, hugging him tightly, she asked him if he was all right.

181

"Yes, I am now that I know you're fine. Christ, honey. Had you not taken those two out, they would have gotten the drop on me. It was all I could do to take care of the five that had tried to kill us." Demi asked if he knew what they were there for. "I didn't stop to ask, but they did have a picture of us on them. And a note, I'm assuming, to leave behind. They were planning to kidnap us."

Demi had dealt with this kind of thing before—someone trying to kidnap her or someone that she loved. Grandma had been the target before, and she'd shot the man when he'd broken into her house to take her. And being here, with these people, Demi had let her guard down.

Alden told her that both men at the gatehouse were dead, a single bullet hole in each of their foreheads.

"Demi?" She looked at Lucian and realized that she'd missed something. "Does this have to do with what happened earlier? In town?"

"Oh no. Nothing like that. The city planner wants to get a bunch of buildings off the books, but he's not willing to part with them one at a time. If we want them, then it's all or nothing." She grinned at Lucian. "You might have to go to the next few city meetings. I might have pissed the man off."

"Might have pissed him off, or you *did* piss him off?" She laughed with him, feeling the stress from today lighten up. "Why don't you tell me what has you so upset about this group of men? I'm thinking that this has happened to you before."

After going home, they had showered off the rest of the afternoon and then got dressed. She sat down on the edge of the bed and tried to think how best to tell him that they'd have to be on guard. He told her to just say it, like she normally would.

"Now that we're all used to having money, we have to be extra careful when we go out. There is always some idiot out there that figures taking a rich person, or someone that they love, is a fast and easy way to make money. It's not. Not the times that it happened to me." He asked her how many. "Five, not counting today. Twice to my grandma, and I haven't any idea how many times before that to her family. But we have to be careful. I think that the people from today were better prepared and equipped than the ones before. They came in a group, with guns, and killed. Kidnappers usually don't. And the reason for it this time is that they don't have an inside man. All the people here are loyal to this family and only this family. It's why we pay them so well."

"What happened before?" She told him, the highlights anyway. "I have a feeling that it was more than you at the mall when someone tried to take you, wasn't it?"

"How they did it isn't as important as that they didn't get me. Had it not been for me carrying a gun, it might have ended badly. As it is, the man is still in prison for shooting a cop, and I'm here to talk about it." She got up and went to the window. "Those two men that worked for us—I'm going to have to do something for their families. I should have taken more precautions with them and us on this."

Demi leaned into him when Lucian came up behind her. He simply held her in his arms while she thought of the lives that had been taken today and why. Money. It seemed that it always came down to money.

"I got a call from the police station. They said that if you want to come and claim Nathan and Astrid's things, you can. There isn't much for either of them. Not even a cell phone."

183

She told Lucian to have them donate or dispose of it. "All right. And the city planner. You want me to go there as my bear and make him do what you want? I will, no problem. In fact, it would be my pleasure to slay this particular dragon for you."

"No, he's going to be all right. Especially when he reads the report from Jamie. He did a little investigating around town, and there are far more things for him to worry about than just a few buildings on the book. The water that goes out to where the building is going to be isn't up to code. Jamie connected his lines to the city lines, and that's as far as he can go for the moment." Lucian asked what would happen if the city guy didn't bring things up to code. "Then Jamie will sue him. And win too. If the city doesn't make it so that he can hook up to the water lines, then Jamie will build his own water plant. After that, he'll sue the city and the planner for the money that he used to make it so he could bring his business out here. A win win for Jamie, and not so much for the city."

Lucian laughed. And even as they made their way down to lunch, he was still laughing. It was funny, really, to see a grown man get such a kick out of someone else's problems. Demi was glad now that she'd told him. After this morning, it was good to have a good laugh.

Chapter 13

Lucian was looking over the rest of the paperwork from the bank when his phone rang. It came in as an unknown, but since he'd not set up the desk type phone yet, he supposed everyone would come up unknown.

"Hello. My name is Micky Mantle. I was wondering if you could tell me if you have any strangers in town." Lucian started to ask the man if he was kidding or he really was named after a famed baseball player. "I'm doing an article for a big newspaper, and we want to see how small towns, such as yours, deal with unwanted strangers."

"I wouldn't know if they were unwanted until I got to know them. Then they'd no longer be a stranger, now would they?" Lucian was sure that he'd taken the man off guard with his answer. "What is it you're writing about? Strangers? That doesn't seem like a very read worthy article. Which paper is this going to be in?"

"It'll be syndicated, so it'll be in all kinds of papers." That wasn't an answer at all, and he told the man that. "What does

185

it matter which paper it is? I'm just trying to get a perspective on what it is your town does with strangers. Until you get to know them."

"As I pointed out before, they're no longer strangers. Why don't you get to the point, and then we can get on with our day?" The man growled. "Buddy, you're going to have to do a great deal better than that, dealing with me. Tell me."

The compulsion was something that Lucian rarely used. But in this case, he thought it was necessary. Either for his family or for the woman that they were hiding. The man fought against Lucian making him tell the truth, but in the end, it was extremely helpful.

"There is a woman that I've been looking for. Her name is Meadow Spring. She is supposed to have killed her entire family. There is a doctor that I've been following who has been trying to say that she had nothing to do with it. I want her to be found guilty of these crimes. And I'm going to make it so she is when I find her." Lucian asked him why he'd made himself judge, jury, and executioner. "Because I'm the only one that cares that she is found guilty, I told you. The rest of the world believes her to be someone that is sick and hurt too badly to stand trial. I'm sure that it's all a lie."

"Is it? So, for the last—what, seven years or so, since the accident, she's been pretending to be this person who plans to get away with it. Doesn't seem very likely if you ask me." The man said he had only been searching for her for six, and he'd not asked him. "No, it's been only six since she was taken out of the hospital and moved around. The murders took place over seven years ago."

"It was seven years, four months, and ten days to be exact. Plus, don't you think you know a great deal about this for a person who doesn't know anything?" Lucian could have told him that he and his wife were looking over everything nightly to help the woman out, but he didn't. Nor did he tell the man that he remembered the murders. "Where is she?"

"Who?" The man growled again, and Lucian couldn't help it; he growled right back at him. "Christ, what the fuck are you? A dog? Just tell me where she is, Meadow Spring."

"No, I'm a bear, and I haven't any idea where she is. And you're going to think this is really funny, but I don't care at all where she might be either." Micky, or whatever his name was, laughed. "You think that's funny?"

"Sure I do. And when I find her, I'm going to make sure that I get all the information I can before I kill her too. You'll see. I'll be famous." Lucian told him what he'd be was dead. "By you? Nah, I'm not worried about you. You're just some fat fuck that doesn't do much of anything but sit behind a big desk and order people around. Just like her old man did. Someone should have taken him out a long time ago."

Lucian felt the hairs on his neck dance, his bear rolling over him in the need to hunt the man down and kill him. But as calmly as he could, and with more compulsion then he'd ever used before, he asked the man if he'd killed the family.

"Of course I did. And that fucking bitch saw my face. I need to end her before I can move on to someone else. Some other family that I want to fuck up their lives. Because as long as they believe she did it, I'm safe. But once she's dead, then all bets are off. But she will die."

Lucian laid the phone in the cradle and sat there. He wasn't sure what he was to do now, and instead of picking up the phone to call the police, he called Demi. She might not know what to do either, but she'd surely know who to call.

187

Lucian was afraid, more than he had been even the other day when they'd been attacked in the woods.

"Demi. Where are you?" She said that she was in the office downtown. "I need for you to come home. Now. I have something that I need to tell you face to face."

"You're scaring me, Lucian. Is it bad?" He said that it was about as bad as it gets. "I'm coming there. Don't do anything stupid."

"Like what?" She told him not to do anything. "I can do that. My mind won't allow me to do much more than to sit here and not piss myself. I have to call in my brothers and get them in on this. My parents should go to the place where Meadow is. To make sure that she's safe."

"Why?" He said he'd explain when she got there. "Lucian, you're scaring me more and more with each passing minute."

"I talked to the killer of Meadow's family." She didn't say anything, but he could feel how shocked she was. "Come here, love. I need to hold you while I tell you about the monster that I just spoke to."

"I'm on my way."

He didn't know what to do but did finally get up out of his chair. As soon as Demi got here, he was going to have his phone number changed and the phone that he'd spoken on destroyed. It was tainted somehow. As soon as he heard someone pull in the driveway, his bear roared out against his skin. Lucian knew he was making him scared too. They all would be after this.

When his brothers were there, Demi sent two more to the nursing home to keep an eye on Meadow. There wasn't any point in all of them being here when she was in town basically alone. As soon as they were all seated, Moses brought in drinks and sandwiches. Lucian wondered, not for the first time, if the man had them in reserve someplace.

After telling them what the two of them had spoken about and what the man had finally told him as it pertained to Meadow, Lucian began to pace the room. Demi had been quiet since she'd arrived, but his brothers had plenty of questions. Mostly it was about the nerve of the caller.

"We have to figure out not only where he called from, but his name." Demi told Pierce that it wasn't necessary for them to have his name right now. "Okay, but I refuse to call him Micky Mantle."

"We can call him Micky Mouse for all I care." Lucian took a deep breath and let it out slowly before speaking again. "I'm sorry. You have no idea how dirty that guy made me feel. And to hear him talk about killing that young woman like she wasn't anything at all made me slightly ill to my stomach."

"Demi, you have to help us. We can't have her hurt." Demi said that she didn't want that either. "All right. What can we do for her? There has to be something."

"We'll bring her here. This would be the safest place for her while that fool is out there." They were all nodding, and he found himself nodding as well. "At least with all of us around, close, then we can keep a better eye on her, as well as watch out for this guy. Because I have no doubt that he will do just as he says. From the crime scenes, I'd say that he had no trouble with murder."

"What about the police? Should we let them know what's going on?" Lucian shook his head at Gannon. "Why not? I mean, they have guns and a force to call on."

"We have bears. And the less people who know about this, the better. I mean, we trust us. I sort of trust the police, but I would bet my life on my family rather than the police in something like this." Demi told him he was right. "But I do wonder about the doctors. Should they know?"

Moses came in, telling Demi she had a phone call. When she left to answer it, Moses asked if they needed anything else. The man was unflappable. He and Bea just rolled with the punches as if they did this sort of thing daily.

"We're fine, thank you." Moses nodded, then turned back to them all as he was leaving the room. "Yes? Something else happen? Please tell me that it's not bad."

"No, sir. But I would like to tell you that in the sub levels of this house, under the basement, is a shelter. It's been there since before the war. The family's wealth and other items were hidden down there when the war was being fought around this town. Even the women folk, my father told me, were hidden down there in case someone tried to take one of them." He smiled. "My father also told me that he and the coloreds, what he called himself, hid down there for a time too. It was part of the underground railroad at one time. Shall I have it cleaned up and stocked, just in the event we need it?"

"Yes, please do that. And if you'd make sure that there are sleeping bags down there, enough for my family and your and Bea's family as well, I'd appreciate it." When he nodded and left, Lucian looked at his family. "I want every one of you to go find the entrance to the place below and make sure you know how to get to it in a hurry. I don't want anyone hurt if it comes to that."

"Mom and Dad too." Lucian nodded.

When Demi came back in the room, she was white as a ghost. Having her sit down, he handed her the small glass of amber liquid that Madden handed him. Demi drank it down

190

in one gulp.

"They're dead." He didn't want to ask her how. He had a feeling that he knew. "The doctors. And their families. They were all killed not an hour ago. Not like the Spring family was, but one was a car accident while the other was carbon monoxide poisoning. They're all dead. We're all on our own here."

Lucian sat with his wife while the rest of them sat quietly. They were in over their heads again. Not like before with just money woes, but with a mass murderer coming to hurt them. Because he would before they'd allow this person to get Meadow.

"Go into town. Bring her back here." Madden and Pierce stood up. "It doesn't matter if you're slick about it. He must know that she's here. The only thing we have going for us right now is whether or not he knows what you guys are."

His brothers left. They were told to bring back Meadow, as well as anything that she had there, things that had been brought with her that she might miss or need. Demi started telling them things that they'd need to do. Treat it like we're about to be kidnapped, she told them.

"No one goes to town alone. We all stay here too. I know that you have jobs and businesses that you're working at, but this has to be first." Lucian asked what he could do. "There are guns in the locked storage room in the basement. It might not get to be a gun fight, but we have to be prepared. Also, there is a button down there. It's bright green. Push it."

"What does it do, honey?" She told him that she'd explain when he got back. All the way to the basement, all he could think about was that someone was going to be fried if they tried to breach the fence.

When he returned, Josiah had come from the dealership.

"Call Jamie and tell him that I need you here. He'll understand that something is wrong if I need to call in the family." Josiah said that he'd do that. "Also, you'll need to stay here too, Josiah. I don't want anyone out where this guy can try and use you against us. He will, I have a feeling. Especially if he starts to get desperate."

By the time his parents were back with Meadow, things had been set up. The green button did electrify the fence, and the gatehouse was now closed as well. Demi handed them each a badge that would get them in and out, but only with their fingerprint. She showed him how to set them up with the computer. It was going to be difficult, Lucian thought, to get Meadow with all these precautions they were taking.

~*~

Josiah nearly fell back when he saw the woman getting out of the car. She was beautiful. Long blonde hair that was braided and hung down her back. Her hands and face, from what he could see, were as delicate looking as she looked. And when they started helping her into the house, carrying her up the stairs, he stared at her for several minutes before someone hit him in the face.

"We can't get her in the house if you're going to stand there with your tongue hanging out." Demi glared harder when he didn't move. "Did you hear me? Get the fuck out of my way."

"She's afraid." Demi told him that they all were. "No, of you. Not afraid really but scared all the same, and she's my mate."

"No fucking shit?" He didn't know how to answer that in an affirmative way, so just moved out of the way and then knelt in front of her wheelchair after the door was closed behind her. "Josiah, are you sure? I mean, I don't know the how of it, but could this be just that you're worried for her?"

"No, she's my mate." He put his hand on hers and pulled his back when she did. "She doesn't like to be touched, does she? Gonna make it kind of hard for us, don't you think?"

He was nervous too, and making jokes was his way of dealing with it. Or talking too much too fast. Putting out his hand, he wanted to tell her who she was to him, but he only waited, telling her what was going on instead of what was on his mind.

"He told my brother that you saw him. Saw his face." She turned and looked at him, and Josiah was startled speechless by the color of her eyes. "You're very beautiful, and the color of your eyes reminds me of the coldest ice on the pond by our home. They're not blue, but not gray either. Just beautiful."

He wondered if she could understand him. No one had told him the extent of her injuries, only that she didn't talk and that she wouldn't walk, even though the muscles in her legs were worked every day. When she finally put her hand into his, Josiah felt like he'd won the grand prize at work. She didn't smile or look at him, but Josiah was all right with this for now.

"We're going to protect you here. This is my brother and his wife's home." Demi said that she'd been here before. "Really? When? I mean, surely that will help, won't it?"

"I don't know, Josiah. It was a long time ago. She came here for Christmas a few times with her parents. I wouldn't have remembered her except for seeing the color of her eyes. I think her father's were the same color."

Meadow looked at Demi and then back at him. It was the

first time that he felt like they'd made a connection, their eyes locking in some sort of understanding of each other.

Josiah told Meadow everything that he could remember from Lucian, and he didn't try and sugar coat it. She was his mate, and while he couldn't lie to her, he wasn't going to have her not be aware of what was going on. Wheeling her into the living room, he sat on the floor in front of her, needing to be as close to her as he could.

When Moses said that dinner was ready, he sat with Meadow in the living room. None of them knew what she ate or how she ate it. Was she able to get a shower alone? Dress herself? The only persons they could ask were dead.

"We'll just have to learn this as we go, I guess. I've never taken care of anyone in a wheelchair before, so this will be a first for all of us." She looked away from him, and his heart hurt a bit. But she was looking at his mom, who had a tray in her hands. "Are you hungry? I am too. Let's see what my mom brought us."

"She's a lovely little thing, isn't she, Josiah? My goodness, and to have gone through too much to get to you." He'd not thought of it that way and told his mom that. "Well, she has to be strong. I mean, someone tried to kill her, and did her entire family. She might need you to help her, but I'd stay out of her way if she has it in her head to take care of business."

Meadow watched him as he put the tray over her lap. He started to stand and help her get up in the chair better, but she did it on her own. That was when he saw the scars on her arm, the ones on her wrist as well. She was looking at him when he turned to look at her face.

"I'm sorry that you were hurt like this." She didn't say anything but did continue to stare at him. "When I find this guy, I'm going to rip his head off and feed it to him. Just so we're clear on that. Unless, of course, you want to do it. I'm all for that as well. You'll see that our parents raised us to think that if someone involved can do the job, male or female, then they should be the ones put in charge."

She ate her mashed potatoes first. The gravy she scooped off and set it aside. There were green beans, which she ate too, but not the broccoli nor the carrots. The sliced ham was eaten, but not with her fork. Instead she picked it up with her fingers and ate it that way. Josiah was laughing when she pushed the corn onto her spoon and ate it with the gravy that she'd set aside.

"I'll have to remember that. No broccoli or carrots, and you like gravy over your vegetables, not the potatoes." Josiah handed her his ham sandwich to see if she would eat it too. It took her a moment to figure it out—her hand, the left one, didn't work nearly as well as the right.

Dad bought them in pie later, and a glass of juice for Meadow. She had to use a straw—again, her hand did not work well enough to hold up a heavy glass. Josiah thought about holding it for her but knew that she'd tell him to fuck off if she could. Josiah had a feeling that she'd been doing for herself for a long time now.

He also figured out that she didn't care for sweets, at least what was brought to them. No apple nor cherry pie, but she did eat the whipped cream off one of the slices. And when he set an orange on her tray, Meadow looked at it as if she hadn't any idea what it was.

"When we were little, there wasn't much money at home. All our gifts were hand made by my mom, and we did the same for the two of them." He started to peel the orange for her, just to give her a taste if he could. "At Christmas we each got an orange, a rare treat for us, and an apple in our stocking. Mom still does that to this day, an apple and an orange at Christmas. Can you smell it?"

She didn't answer him, of course, but she did take a small bite of the fruit. When she opened her mouth again, he put small pieces up for her to take from him. He didn't want her to get it all over her. Sharing the fruit with her, he told her about himself, what he was doing, and the house that he'd just gotten.

"It's being renovated now. I have to think if I want an elevator in it or not. If we don't have one yet, we'll have one put in. I'll have to ask Demi and Lucian, of course—they're helping us out with the work being done on the house." He thought about his car too, and that it was much too small for a wheelchair. "We'll go shopping for a bigger car when this is over. That guy, he's going to get his ass kicked all over the place when he gets around to coming here."

"I'd like to show her a picture, Josiah. There are six pictures in her file, all of them men that were talked to after the murders. And since she couldn't be asked, no one ever pointed the finger at anyone else but her." Demi handed it to him. "She's doing things with you that she hadn't before. She would never let anyone help her, and she wasn't to be touched. You've done both in the few minutes that you've been together. If you'd show her the picture, we'll see who we might be dealing with. I'm only going to show her one at a time, however."

He looked at his mate. She was staring at Demi in a familiar way. Josiah had a feeling that's what she did to everyone she first met, trying to place them in her mind until she either trusted them or didn't.

"This is a picture of one of the men that might be coming here, Meadow." She looked at him. "I'm going to show you a picture of someone. I don't know what you'll do if this is the man you saw in your home that night, but it would help us to know who we're dealing with, all right?"

Nothing. But it was no less than he expected. Slowly he raised the picture up from in front of him to let her see a little of it at a time. When he had it upright, she only stared at it then turned away again. Josiah thought that could mean anything. He looked at Demi, asking her about what sort of reaction she was expecting.

"I have no idea. But I guess I thought that if it was him, she'd be afraid. Or at the very least show fear on her face." Josiah said that might not happen either, even after showing her all of them. "No. It might not, but we have to try. With a name, we can certainly figure out what sort of person we're dealing with. If he has a record or not. What his MO might be like on other murders. He was just too good at the murders. It was too planned for him to have never done this before. Right?"

"I guess." Meadow put out her hand and Demi handed her the picture again. But she looked at it and put it down before putting out her hand again. Demi put the next picture in her hand. Neither of them said a word. "I don't think that's him either. And I think that she understands us more than that doctor told us she did. He seemed to think she was sort of brain damaged. I don't think so."

"I think you're right." The third picture got a reaction, but not what they had expected. Demi told him that it was of the doctor, Doctor Judson Little. Meadow had smiled. Then the fourth and fifth picture got no reaction. "Last one. It doesn't mean that it's the last one I'll show her, but the last one in her file. A Doctor Little gathered these up, the file said, when the trial was over."

Meadow screamed. It brought his entire family running when she did that. Her tears tore at Josiah, and he tried to hold her. But she wasn't having any of it. He was ready to give up on trying when his dad said that he had to hold her, to show her that they would never harm her. So, fighting his way past her fists and hands, he put his arms around her, lifted her from the chair, and held her in his arms.

Sitting with her on the couch, he held her until she calmed down. It hurt him to have done this to her, but at least it was over. Demi said that they had a name now, one that they could work with, and it would go a long way in catching the bastard. When he wrapped a coverlet over them both, Josiah talked softly to Meadow, telling her how sorry he was that he'd done that. He stopped when he heard her whispering.

"Don't move, you fucking cunt. I will kill you like the rest of them if you do." Josiah called for Lucian via their link and told him what she was saying. Demi and he came in with a recorder and handed it to Josiah. "You should have seen them bleeding. The blood will be on the walls for the rest of your very short life, do you hear me? When I'm finished here, I'm going to rob this house of everything here. Then set it on fire. You never know what sort of DNA I might have left behind."

"She's talking about the murderer. He talked to her." Demi said that it appeared so. "Do you think that he talked to the rest of the victims? That he didn't care if he talked to them because he knew they were all going to die?"

"He didn't burn down the house." He looked at Meadow

198

when she spoke to him. "He didn't burn down the house because someone knocked on the door. He was frightened off. Someone scared him into leaving me there to die. I wish that he'd killed me."

Meadow started crying, and he held her tightly in his arms. She was aware, his mind told him. Not only that, but she was remembering things since she was shown the picture. Or, she remembered all along and now trusted that she was going to get help. Either way, he wasn't sure this was a good thing. Now she would be able to point the finger, as everyone had wanted her to do from the beginning.

"I don't want you to die, Meadow. You're my mate. Do you know what that means?" She shook her head and he smiled. "I'll tell you, but you have to look at me."

She did, and he was slightly afraid. Meadow didn't like to be told what to do. Laughing, he told her that he was only joking, but he did like looking at her. She laid her head back on his shoulder then and said nothing more.

"You're my other half. My wife, by our laws. I won't make you do anything, ever, that you don't want to do, but I will protect you with my life. All my family will." She looked at him then and told him that her family hadn't been able to protect her and her little brother. "No, and I'm profoundly sorry about that. But we're bears, and we protect what is our family."

"I lost them all that night. Everyone that meant anything to me. But Danny, he was only six years old. He'd be fourteen now if that man hadn't killed him." Josiah said he wouldn't wish for her to die. "I'm alone. No matter what you say, I'm all alone, and everyone believes that I killed them all."

"I don't." Meadow looked at him, and Josiah could see

199

that she wasn't sure to believe him or not. "I know that you didn't kill them, Meadow. My family believes that as well. And we're going to make sure that the world knows it too."

"How?" Josiah told her that he didn't know, hadn't a clue, but he'd do it. "I don't know why he did that to us. Why? Why would he kill my family? They were good to everyone."

"I don't know, honey. But I will promise you this. When we find him, and we will, I'll straight up ask him. Not that it matters." She asked him why. "Because the fucker is going to die anyway. You'll see."

Before You Go...

HELP AN AUTHOR

write a review

THANK YOU!

Share your voice and help guide other readers to these wonderful books. Even if it's only a line or two your reviews help readers discover the author's books so they can continue creating stories that you'll love. Login to your favorite retailer and leave a review. Thank you.

AWARD WINNING, BESTSELLING AUTHOR

Kathi Barton, winner of the Pinnacle Book Achievement award as well as a best-selling author on Amazon and All Romance books, lives in Nashport, Ohio with her husband Paul. When not creating new worlds and romance, Kathi and her husband enjoy camping and going to auctions. She can also be seen at county fairs with her husband who is an artist and potter.

Her muse, a cross between Jimmy Stewart and Hugh Jackman, brings her stories to life for her readers in a way that has them coming back time and again for more. Her favorite genre is paranormal romance with a great deal of spice. You can visit Kathi online and drop her an email if you'd like. She loves hearing from her fans. aaronskiss@gmail.com.

Follow Kathi on her blog: http://kathisbartonauthor.blogspot.com/